Stolen Moments
A World Beyond

By Michelle Howard
Published by MH Publications

Also by Michelle Howard

A Novel of the Dracol
Rylin's Fire
Relentless Fire
Frost Fire
Secret Fire

Assassins Guild
The Unexpected Bonding Vow
Claiming His Unexpected Baby
His Unexpected Mate

A World Beyond
Torkel's Chosen
Torkels Auserwählte
Arak's Love
Arak's Liebe
Lindsey's Rescue
Kyele's Passion

Rydak's Fall
Jaron's Promise
V'hor's Nestmate
Stolen Moments
Bane's Heart
Nikol's Surrender

Cyborg Redemption
His Cold Kiss
Her Cold Heart

Ghost Unit
Raging Tempest
Craving Love

Le Cœur dans les étoiles
Union à tout prix
Amour à toute épreuve

Liebe in den Sternen
Animalische Begierde
Einzigartige Liebe

Love in the Stars
Mating Urge
Love Like No Other

Magical Lovers
Djinn Lover
Wicked Lover
Wild Lover

The Vassi Contact
As Darkness Spreads
As Dawn Rises

Un roman de L'univers Dracol
La Flamme de Rylin
La Flamme verte
La Flamme de glace

Un Roman di Dracol
il fuoco di Rylin
Fuoco Implacabile
Fuoco di Ghiaccio

Warlord Series
Honor Bound
The Overlord's Heir
A King's Revenge
Rise of the Shadow Warriors
A Warlord's Heart
Unexpected Bride
Unleashing A Warrior

Wired
Wired for Love

Standalone
No Reason To Run
Project Genesis

Watch for more at www.michellehowardwrites.com.

For All Time

A World Beyond Novella

By Michelle Howard

Published by MH Publications

Chapter 1

The front door opened and closed. Anticipation sizzled through Joni as she settled back on the bed, adjusting her clothing for the best effect. Steps came down the hall, paused then continued. Holding her breath, she waited as the knob turned then the bedroom door opened. A large shadowy form stepped into the room and flicked the wall switch. The table lights next to the bed gave off a dim glow.

"Joni?" He scanned the room until he spotted her and froze.

Exactly the reaction she had hoped for.

"I'm glad you're home." Joni had taken extra special care with her appearance tonight. The body of the corset in blinding white was a stark contrast to the red hair she knew fascinated her Chosen. Lace discretely covered her nipples, matching the same design on the front panel of her white bikinis.

"Did you miss me?" Kyele taunted as he regained his composure and slowly began to undress out of his uniform.

He'd only been at a training for most of the day. But she *had* missed him. Joni's breath caught in the back of her throat. Sometimes she forgot how hot he was when removing his clothing. First, the knives from his thigh sheaths were placed on the bedside table. Next, he removed the laser holstered at his hip and toed off his well-worn boots. Buttons on his high collared black shirt were undone with no signs of haste, then his hands lowered to the flap of his matching cargo pants and paused. His dark brows lifted in inquiry and she realized he wouldn't finish until she answered.

"I did miss certain parts." She kept her voice low and teasing, gaze on the part of him she missed the most.

Green eyes glittered in pleasure, flickers of passion blooming to life. Joni had big plans for Kyele. He'd been unusually quiet after her announcement about being pregnant. That had been two days ago. Two days of her worrying if he now had second thoughts about having a baby.

Kyele shrugged his broad shoulders and the shirt fluttered to the floor. He hooked his thumbs at the waist of his pants and lowered them without a hint of shyness. Tanned skin from head to toe layered over rippling muscles. Not even the jagged scar on the left side of his face could take away from his appeal.

Completely naked, he made his way toward their bed and stretched out on his back. She caught his smug grin before he masked his expression to one of dark neutrality. Of course, he could be smug. She didn't hide the effect he had on her. Joni fucking loved him and didn't care who knew it.

Kyele's grin was wolfish as he reached down and stroked himself from base to tip. "So quiet now. What do you want, Earthling?"

"You know what I want," Joni growled, crawling across the bed on her knees toward him.

The corners of his lips twitched and there was no mistaking the humor glinting in his gaze. His smirk defined sexy and Joni rejoiced in the fact he belonged to her. Every delicious inch.

Kyele tilted his dark head to the side, eyeing her with a smoldering glance. "Why don't you remind me?"

She did better. Joni lowered her head before he could react and mouthed the round head of his thick erection. Kyele shuddered. With her gaze on his face as she sucked him deep, there was no missing the lust that gleamed in the green depths. Her thighs grew embarrassingly damp as desire warmed her middle. There would never be a day she tired of wanting him.

He ripped her corset down the middle. Rough hands burrowed into the loose waves of her hair and tugged. Tiny stings tickled her scalp. Joni moaned and laved his shaft with her tongue. The musky scent of him filled her nostrils, his taste familiar and masculine.

"You are trying to undo me, Earthling."

Kyele's voice was a rasp against her senses. His thighs grew taut, fingers now locked around the strands of her hair as he guided her head up and down in a manner they both enjoyed. Joni because of the control he exhibited by never going too far and hurting her, Kyele because he'd discovered giving blowjobs increased her arousal.

Another groan warned of his impending climax. Joni smiled around his thickness and eased up the sucking pressure. When he growled and tried to lead her back with a firm hand to the back of the head, Joni chuckled and pulled away. She patted his inner leg. "Not yet. We're celebrating."

"Celebrating?" Curiosity and wariness layered the deep voice rich with his lingering desire.

Joni swung her leg over and straddled his lap. The shaft between her thighs twitched, rubbing in exactly the right spot. She gasped and arched her back. Kyele clasped her waist and rocked her back and forth. Joni locked her legs about his hips to still the motion guaranteed to push her right into a devastating orgasm.

"Yes, celebrating. I visited Dr. Maku today." Just thinking about what the medic for the Jutak team shared gave Joni a tiny thrill. A little bit of fear as well, if she was honest.

Kyele's fingers tightened with brutal force on her waist. His face grew serious. "Is something wrong with the baby?"

Joni flinched and eased up to her haunches to relieve the painful grip. Kyele's fingers gentled instantly, going into a soft stroking motion to erase the minute pain he'd caused. "My apologies, Joni. What did Maku say?"

His intense gaze stayed on her face, the look reflecting a dash of fear. It was the fear that soothed Joni's own nerves.

***

Kyele tried to hide it, but it was never far from his thoughts that something could take Joni from him. He'd lived so long with the idea he'd never find a woman able to love him as he was. Full of darkness, and not fully Enotian. His legacy was one of death and a mass killing so violent the memory of the brutality enacted carried a weight of warning to others to this day.

General Azar of the Spectar was his papan and one would be hard pressed to find a more savage opponent. The world of Spectar had once warred hard and often, striking a deep seeded root of fear for any who sought to go against them.

"We're having a boy!"

His lack of immediate reaction proved how far into his thoughts Kyele had gone. He jolted when the words actually penetrated.

He jerked up, cradling his Chosen in his lap and stared. Her happy grin had fallen and now she chewed her bottom lip. He didn't like the sign of nerves. Joni was the only one who didn't fear him and he'd never do anything to change that. He kept one hand at her lower back, supporting her weight and used the other to tip her face up to his. "Tell me again."

He didn't care if he barked the command. His heart thundered in his chest as he waited for her answer.

"The baby. It's a boy according to Dr. Maku. I thought it was too soon to tell but apparently you all can know right away."

Kyele hated the tremor in the statement but still couldn't speak as he stared into the worried amber eyes watching him closely. After much pleading, he'd given in to Joni because she wished to carry a child at the same time as her friend Sylvie. The Earth women found one another at a slave auction and became close friends despite their situation.

"Are you angry?" Joni leaned forward and braced her hands on his shoulders. Hard nipples stabbed at his chest, reminding him of what they'd been doing before she dropped her news on him.

Was he happy? Kyele didn't answer right away. Having a Chosen was a novelty that had yet to settle in. Maybe never would. As a result, he hadn't thought in terms of children. Ever. But as much as he wanted to pretend otherwise it was a reality. He was going to have a son. The image of a rounded Joni, plump with a child they created together overlaid the inquisitive face in front of him and Kyele's heart took flight. But not in pleasure.

"What if something happens to you?"

What if he lost her? Would fate cruelly snatch this newly found love away from him?

Joni cupped his clenched jaw. "Nothing's going to happen to me."

Kyele bit back the need to recite all the ways females died, including birthing a baby.

Her brows lowered and her back stiffened. "I'm getting the feeling you are *not* pleased with this."

She struggled in his lap, attempting to move away. Kyele held her in place easily. He wished he could say what she wanted to hear. He wanted to be jubilant, but how could he when death hovered over his shoulders every waking moment? His heart hammered out a frantic beat. Joni's death would shove Kyele back into the void of loneliness he'd existed in before the day he and his teammates had rescued her.

Kyele clutched Joni close, almost crushing her with the force of his hold. He spoke words he'd never imagined he'd say aloud to anyone. "I'm scared, Earthling."

Puffs of breath hit his neck. The scent of fresh cleanser wafted from the hair he buried his face in. His eyes burned as he closed them then snapped them back open when flashes of a dead Joni played in his mind.

"Kyyy." She dragged out the shortened name only she used for him on a soft sigh then ran her hands over the curve of his shoulders and back. The touch did nothing to lessen the impact of her news. His nerves were fucked. "You're not going to lose me. I haven't fully trained you yet."

An unexpected snort of amusement escaped him. Leave it to Joni to shatter the moment with humor. "Train me? A dedicated Jutak warrior?"

"Pfft." She pulled back from his hold, only succeeding because he allowed it. Joni pressed a finger to his lips and her expression turned serious. "No negative talk. We're having a baby and I'm excited to begin this phase of family life with you."

Family. Joni was his family. His shifted his gaze to her flat stomach. The baby would be his family. He smoothed a section of red-gold hair from her face, the curls bouncing then slipping forward again. "If you seek to leave me, I will hunt you to the ends of this world and the next."

Joni grinned and tugged at his hair. "How about we get back to celebrating our good fortune?"

Distraction. She wanted to distract him from the dark thoughts that still lingered at the back of his mind. Only time would ease his fear. Kyele rolled Joni onto her back and hunched over her. Pink nipples taunted. He ran a hand down her side before going back up and placing a palm over the fullness of a plump breast.

"Mmm." Her lashes fluttered, lips pursed in pleasure.

Kyele lowered his weight to her body with a rough glide. Curves aligned to the muscled plains of his frame. Familiar. Welcome. No more talk of death. He needed to connect with his Chosen. He planted teasing kisses along the side of her face, lips. Claws raked over his back, but he continued his path down her throat, sucking lightly as he went. Long slim legs entwined his hips as Joni used her heels to prod him faster.

"Don't play with me, buddy. You know what I want." She swiveled her hips around, grinding their groins together in case he missed her meaning.

Laughter slipped free. She was sweetness and light but with a sharp edge. He snapped her underwear with a flick of his fingers. Too bad he had no intentions of going faster. "I know exactly what you want, Earthling."

Kyele took his time kissing every inch of the body beneath him, flicking the beaded belly ring. Golden lean muscles went taut as he stroked a sleek hip, a testament to the training she maintained with rigid focus. His Joni had been a victim once, enslaved during a process meant to ensure a happy future. She worked out diligently to prevent ever being that helpless again.

Sliding down between her thighs, he forced her legs to unlock and held them spread aloft. Joni's squeal brought a wicked grin to his face. Smiling was a daily occurrence with his Chosen. Her humor and brightness balanced the dark intensity he battled internally. Proving he deserved her love was a life goal.

"Hold strong, little Earthling, I've yet to begin."

As expected, the taunt caused her to snarl and struggle. She tried to push away from him but Kyele stilled her efforts with ease. Gripping her calves tight, he lowered his head to the apex of her thighs. The wet center of her with the thin strip of bright red curls called to him. One long lick had her arching, fingers latching on to his hair. He did it again, loving the taste of her. Feminine musk, sweetness and all Joni. Kyele would know her blindfolded.

"Ky-ele, don't tease."

He nuzzled her warmth and did more than tease. He licked, tongued and sucked until the folds of her sex swelled and glistened with the creamy evidence of her enjoyment. He continued to work her, mixing nips to the tiny bud with gentle nibbles. All too soon her pleas became broken cries and gasps.

Kyele's hard shaft was one big ache he wanted to grind into the sheets. When he sensed her on the cusp of crossing over, Kyele stopped and lifted.

Face flushed, Joni met his gaze with parted lips and eyes of amber narrowed to slits. "My turn?"

She made no attempts to hide the hunger and eagerness in getting her mouth on him, but Kyele knew he'd never last. He stroked his length, the thick weight pulsing in his hand. The moment her hot tongue touched him again, he'd be done. He wanted to come deep inside her. "Not this time."

"Scared?" She stretched her arms above her head, fiery red hair an explosion over their pillows as she arched to put her body fully on display.

Kyele eased her legs down and leaned over her. With his arms braced by her shoulders, he loomed over her. "You would like to believe that."

He nudged her entrance with the head of his erection, dipping in and out, coating himself until the tip gleamed. Joni rocked on a moan and thrust her hips up. The action served to slide him in deeper. Wet heat. Sucking, snug grip. Nothing and no one felt like Joni.

Kyele growled and gave up all pretense of dragging this out. He started fast with steady pumps which left the both of them covered in a sheen of sweat. The room echoed with the sounds of their passion. Rhythmic pulses fluttered up and down his cock as he labored for breath. A quick glance revealed Joni about to crest. Her moans came louder and louder, strumming his own desire higher.

"Harder, Kyele. Harder."

He powered forth, teeth gritted and neck strained. Joni reached for him and pulled him down until their slick chests rubbed together. Frantic, he pounded into her depths, sensations rolling down his spine, leaving him choking out each breath. His sac drew up as he burned for release. *Not yet.*

He leaned up and drove into her harder. "Mine. My Joni."

"Yes! Yes! I'm coming!"

Her legs came back up and locked about his waist. Kyele fell forward, planted one hand by her head to watch. It was a glorious sight. Joni's neck bent back, dark splotches of red spread across her throat and chest, nipples a deep berry color. Below, her inner muscles became a vise and clamped down on him making it difficult to move but Kyele grabbed one of her thighs and pushed her knee back while slamming his hips forward. Joni screamed.

Blinding lights exploded behind his eyelids. Coming at the same time as Joni added indescribable textures to their sex sharing. Unable to stay upright, Kyele collapsed on her, hips on automaton as he rode the wave of her orgasm. Face on the pillow beside her head, Kyele groaned over and over as he spurted. Beneath him, her body trembled and twitched. He found himself mumbling her name over and over. There were no other words. His mind was blank.

Soft fingers brushed the hair from his temple. "You're the best thing to ever happen to me, Kyele Bastien."

He gathered her close, rolling them to the side with Joni's weight settled in front of him. "Thank you for choosing me."

Her hand reached back to rub his hip, the tension in her body lessening until she slept. Kyele stayed up long past Joni nodding off. He slid his hand to her flat belly. A son.

Chapter 2

6 weeks later

Kyele staggered into the living area after another bout in the cleansing room due to his upset stomach. Heat rolled through his body in random waves, leaving his skin damp and flushed.

"You look awful," Joni gasped when he entered.

Meanwhile, she glowed. The early stages of pregnancy had only enhanced the beauty of his Chosen. Her vibrant red hair with streaks of gold seemed to have gained more vitality if possible, her amber eyes sparkling like they contained a secret.

"I've told Torkel to pull me from any training. Stefin will lead Team Two if they go out before I am recovered."

At the mention of the leadership change, Joni slumped to the sofa lounge. "Oh no. It's my fault. It never crossed my mind you'd end up with morning sickness. It's only been a couple of weeks since I told you. You must hate this pregnancy."

He did. The sickness started a day or two after he'd learned she carried his baby. They were only in the early stages and Kyele had never been more miserable in his life. He took in Joni's dejected pose. It wasn't his Chosen's fault though. She looked lost as she wrapped a blanket about her shoulders and huddled on their sofa. The hem of her silver dress rose, revealing golden limbs as she tucked them beneath her hips.

His fists clenched. He couldn't let her believe what she did. "No."

Joni's head snapped up, confusion brightening her golden eyes. Kyele crossed the room and sat on the sofa, pulling an unresisting Joni onto his lap. She curled into his chest with a relieved cry, her arms going about his neck. Kyele held her close, burying his face in the thick red waves about her shoulders.

"I will never regret you carrying our child."

"Even if you're sick?" Kyele hesitated and Joni jerked back to glare at him. "Kyele!"

Sickness wasn't common for life on Enotia and he couldn't recollect being ill a single day in his life before. Unfortunately, the medic said there was no cure and Kyele would have to wait it out. Perspiration built on his forehead. He forced a smile to his trembling lips and lied. "Being sick isn't that bad."

It was worth it to see the relief filling Joni's gaze as she jumped from his lap. The rocking sensation didn't agree with his stomach but Kyele pressed a hand to his midsection and held back a groan as the world tipped around him.

"Sylvie and Faye want to meet for the morning meal. Now that you're not leaving you can join us."

Kyele weighed the idea of going back to bed in hopes of recovering from whatever Earth curse she'd given him or spending time with his Chosen. Joni won out easily.

As he stood, Joni danced around him then linked her elbow through his on a chuckle. She leaned her head back to see his face, her eyes full of glee. "I'm glad we get to be together, Kyele."

She had odd ways, his Chosen, but never did he doubt her love for him. The trip to the lower level was uneventful for which Kyele gave thanks. At any moment his turbulent stomach seemed ready to revolt.

Voices ebbed and flowed with a laugh here and there the second they crossed the threshold. Scattered about were various members from Team One and Team Three. Joni headed straight for the table where her friends Sylvie and Faye from Earth sat. Soon she was engrossed in conversation about babies and pregnancy.

If Kyele had thought his decision through, he would have realized eating in the common area wasn't the best idea. The smells and sights of the food on everyone's plate played havoc with his control. He shoved his own plate, a congealed nightmare, far across the table, ignoring Arak's snort. He'd kill his teammate. Later. Right now he wasn't sure if he wasn't the one about to die.

***

Joni's mouth turned down at Kyele's muffled groan as he moved his plate away. The green tint to his usually tanned tones spoke loud and clear to how bad he felt. He turned from the table and arranged his face in her neck, puffs of air wisping over her skin.

"Are you sniffing me?

"No, I'm breathing you," he replied with an added squeeze around her waist. Joni melted. His words were sweet albeit strange.

"I'm sorry you have my morning sickness," she said. And she was. What were the odds the traditional pregnancy illness would strike him and not her?

"All day," he corrected, pulling back so she could see his scowl.

Joni was mid-laugh when Jaron interrupted from the other end of the table. "Is he contagious?"

Arak and Torkel straightened in their seats, avid gazes pinned to her and Kyele as if they carried a plague.

"Morning sickness isn't contagious, jerk." Faye shot Jaron a look which spoke volumes.

He squinted at her in doubt and exaggerated leaning away when Kyele turned a dark stare in his direction. At times like this, it was hard for Joni to remember Jaron led a fully competent team of soldiers in addition to being a master at communications.

"It's a condition that afflicts women when they're pregnant." Joni decided to share.

"Not true," Arak declared. Fear flashed across his face. He glanced nervously at his expecting mate and Chosen seated beside him. "Is it, Sylvie?"

Sylvie, her bestie, was pregnant and a little farther along than Joni in her pregnancy—minus the morning sickness. She winked at Joni and soothed Arak with a hand stroking his dark wavy hair. "Some women do suffer in the beginning. I'm lucky, I didn't."

Kyele's head hit Joni's shoulder on another muffled groan and she wrapped her arms about his middle in an effort to ease his illness with her strength and love.

"Why?" Torkel asked as he tightened his hold on Faye, one large palm almost covering the entire bump beneath her shirt. The Unit Leader for the elite soldiers was petrified at the news of Faye's pregnancy and constantly consulted the medic on her condition. Joni was sure he'd follow Faye everywhere if his duties and responsibilities didn't keep him busy.

"It's an Earth thing," Joni said. "I didn't get it either."

Jaron shivered. "I'm glad we're not on Earth. It doesn't sound like a pleasant place at all."

A knife flew across the table and landed with a thud, the tip burying itself strong enough the handle quivered. Jaron jumped to his feet. "Damn it, Kyele!"

Joni laughed as did the others. Kyele didn't budge from his resting place against her and she wasn't sure how he'd thrown the knife without her detecting him moving. "You're upsetting, Joni."

The Team One Leader instantly turned toward her, remorse darkening his blue gaze. Ever since the woman he'd brought to Enotia had left, he'd been off. Not quite himself. Jaron ran a hand through his short blond hair. "I was joking, Joni."

Arak growled.

Jaron rolled his eyes. "My apologies to all of the Earth women. Who," he added, "seem to be growing here on Enotia."

Joni threw her bread at him. She might not have Kyele's unnatural skills with a blade...yet, but she definitely hit what she aimed for. Jaron caught the bread before impact and shot her a glare as he bit it which had her reluctantly chuckling.

"You'd make an excellent Jutak warrior, Joni." His easy going nature was one of the reasons everyone liked Jaron, but Joni sensed trouble brewed beyond the fun-loving façade. She hoped it wasn't because of the Bounty Retriever who'd left. Her fervent hope was for the blond, blue-eyed prankster to make things work with Sasha. The Bounty Retriever obviously had strong feelings for him and vice versa.

"I need to run reports for the meeting later." Jaron saluted their table and left.

"I can't believe we're all going to have our babies close together." Sylvie beamed at her half-shifter mate.

According to Dr. Maku, Faye would give birth first, then Sylvie and Joni last. She'd get to see how the other ladies handled the experience and hoped the Enotians believed in lots of numbing drugs.

Otherwise, she would hold it over Kyele's head.

Chapter 3

2 weeks later

"You look better, Kyele."

Torkel's words greeted Kyele as soon as he dropped into his seat in the conference room. Everyone at the table gave him amused smirks, knowing how bad he'd suffered over the last weeks from the Earth malady for pregnant women. Only instead of Joni being ill, it was Kyele who had suffered.

"I'm fully recovered."

After consulting Dr. Maku, Kyele had been pulled from active duty during that time until he wasn't in danger of losing his stomach. Or passing out from a dizzy spell which had only happened once. Unfortunately once was enough as it scared Joni to the point she'd contacted Torkel and the medic and Kyele had been temporarily sidelined. In truth it was a relief not to worry he'd jeopardize a mission due to his condition.

"Good." Another smile and Torkel started the meeting by directing everyone's attention to the holo screen.

Kyele listened, excitement growing as he realized his team would be the one going out.

"Does everyone understand the details?" Torkel asked at the end.

Nods around the room. Jaron's fingers flew over the data pad in his hand. "All information has been sent to Team Two."

"Good." Torkel wrapped everything up then added, "Kyele, the sooner you leave the better. The Commander wants this handled quickly."

A rebel faction on a peaceful world sounded simple, but Kyele knew even the most basic missions could turn into a fuck all with devastating results. "I'll arrange transport and we'll leave within the hour."

He eyed Stefin, Creed, Savin and Markus, the other members on his team and received confirmations from each. Kyele rose eager to return to work. First, he needed to inform Joni.

He found her in the training room running on a glider. Dressed in tiny black shorts that exposed the bottom half of her butt cheeks and a skimpy blue top that stopped directly beneath her breasts, it was hard to believe she was carrying their baby. Strapped to each thigh were the knives she'd stolen from a Marenian during her escape from a slave auction. Knives she'd become very good at handling much to Kyele's surprise.

Her red ponytail swished back and forth across her shoulder blades like a burning flame as she slowed. Kyele leaned against the wall and crossed his arms over his chest to wait. Joni was the strongest woman to cross his path. Or maybe he hadn't spent enough time around other females. The scar on his face and his distant manner prohibited him having more experience around them. Although according to Joni, those two things made him hotter in her estimation.

His breath caught at the memory. It was the little things she said to him that kept Kyele enthralled. Joni wasn't just a woman of words, she was one of action and they all pointed to her love for him time and time again. It was a novel concept that took some getting used to, but Kyele would be lying if he didn't admit how much it meant to him. Joni knew him as no other did. She accepted his dark half and never let it diminish what was between them.

While the mechanical voice counted down the sequence on her cool down, she reached for the drying cloth hanging off the handles. When the machine stopped, she stepped down, patting her face dry. It took a moment for her to notice him. Amber gold eyes widened before her mouth stretched into a welcoming grin. "Kyele!"

His lips twitched despite attempting to maintain a stern demeanor. Geile and his brother Gregir entered the training room behind Kyele, inclining their heads to Joni as they passed.

Joni strode toward him, swaying hips and a sexy glint in her gaze. His cock throbbed, responding as usual to the sight of his Chosen. She draped her arms about his shoulders and leaned her weight into him, knowing he'd brace and hold her. Which he did.

"Were you looking for me?"

He stroked his hands up and down her hips. "Yes. I'm leaving shortly and wanted to let you know. I won't be back until later tonight."

She played with the hair at the back of his neck, her touch sending tingles down his spine. If there was more time, he'd carry her back to their place and thoroughly worship her body.

When she lifted slightly to kiss his chin, he hooked an arm beneath her butt and helped. The contact pushed them into closer proximity if possible.

"Hurry back," she whispered, fingers trailing over the scar on his face.

A scar he'd kept as a lesson and reminder of his past.

Not willing to settle for such a timid goodbye, Kyele shifted one hand to the back of Joni's head and slanted his mouth over hers. Soft and teasing, she immediately tangled her tongue with his on a rich moan. They kissed, deep, frantic then slow and wicked.

From somewhere off to the side hoots and cheers went up. Joni pulled back and laughed against his lips. Kyele sent a glare over her shoulder at Arak who'd joined Geile and Gregir in their work out.

***

Holding onto Kyele, Joni glanced over her shoulder and snorted in amusement at the three Jutak warriors staring with teasing smiles. "Are you going with Team Two or the brothers?"

Kyele lowered her to her feet and made sure she was steady before stepping back. "Torkel wants all of Team Two on this."

Joni nodded and kept her expression neutral. She hoped. Every time the teams left she worried for him but it was his job and he was damn good at it. "No dizziness? Queasy stomach?"

He'd gone to see the team medic yet she felt the need to confirm everything was fine with him. She was still concerned he might have lingering effects from the morning sickness. If anything happened to Kyele, Joni wasn't sure how she'd react. He was her compass, her home plate in the alien world she found herself in.

"Joni, Maku cleared me." He gripped her upper arms as he spoke the words clearly and Joni realized she might not have hidden her worries as well as she thought.

She placed a hand on her stomach where their baby grew. She'd begged and pleaded with Kyele to start a family pretty soon after they'd gone through presentation and become legally Chosen to one another. She countered his reluctance with assured confidence but deep inside, she was scared. This was a new and exciting thing for her. For them. But she definitely didn't want to do it alone.

"Joni?" Kyele knuckled her chin, a glimpse of confusion in the green eyes she loved.

Firming her shoulders, she dropped her hand and waved at him. "I'm fine. I'll go shopping. I know it's too early, but I want to see if Enotia does maternity wear as well as they do the daily wear."

Joni freely admitted she had an addiction to the many clothing styles available at the market place. The range of colors, fabrics and styles from vendors of various planets encompassed a range that appealed to her adventurous spirit.

Kyele studied her for one long minute then let go and moved away. At the door, he paused and turned back. "Don't go alone."

Joni rolled her eyes. "You forget I'm stronger than I look and I've been training with super soldiers."

The others snickered behind her. Kyele didn't. His brows lowered in a forbidding scowl, a significant dip of his gaze to her waist and she knew what he meant. "I'll be careful, Kyele."

"I can accept that."

Joni watched his sexy glide as he left, the air of danger surrounding him ever present. The boots, black shirt and matching military pants really did it for her. The weapons strapped all over his body, including the knives at his thighs only made him hotter.

Yes, she was lucky indeed. On that note, she waved at the guys and left the training room. If she hurried, she could shower and dress with time to convince the ladies to shop with her.

By the time Joni was ready, she'd spent more time than she wanted. Her first stop was Lissi's. She knocked on her door but Lissi's Chosen, Rydak, answered cuddling his sleeping son on his bare chest and his daughter twined about his right leg. Joni allowed herself the necessary time to appreciate all of the masculine beauty on display before she spoke, "Is Lissi about?"

"She is resting." He said it in a lowered voice after a cautious glance over his shoulder and Joni once more found herself contemplating how someone as shy as Torkel's sister managed to end up with the scary, quiet yet ridiculously beautiful leader of Team Three.

In any event, Lissi was fortunate since it seemed like Rydak was on daddy duty. "Alright."

Next up was Faye's door only to have Torkel tell Joni she was out visiting his maman, Shaya. A flick of her fingers in farewell and Joni bounced down to the floor where Sylvie lived with Arak. Her bestie had to be available.

Her knock was answered immediately by the half-shifter Jutak. His dark hair was tousled and a red flush stained his cheeks. Slight scratches marred his shirtless chest.

"Joni." Was all he managed as she lightly shoved him to the side and let herself in.

Sylvie sat on the floor, her back against a lounger wearing nothing but an overlarge man's shirt. Arak's obviously. Joni propped her hands on her hips and hesitated. They'd obviously finished or were starting to make out. "I came to invite you shopping, but you're getting all lovey-dovey with your officer kitty cat."

Her friend didn't look the least bit remorseful at being caught and clapped both hands to her belly. "Pregnancy has officially kicked in. One word—hormones. My mate's shifter hormones, pregnancy hormones...there are hormones everywhere, Joni and I'm feeling all of them."

Dropping her hands to her side, Joni chuckled. Sylvie *was* showing. A nice round mini-ball when yesterday there had only been a slight curve. "You have a baby belly!"

Joni raced across the room and dropped to her knees beside her. Sylvie grabbed one of Joni's hands and settled it high on the upper swell. "Feel."

A determined thump tapped against her palm. Joni's head snapped up and their gazes locked. Tears burned, but she swallowed them back. "A kick?"

Sylvie nodded then blubbered, "It started first thing this morning after my belly popped and hasn't stopped."

Arak came over and slid behind his mate, her weight cradled between his spread legs. His arms came around her, hands protectively cupping her stomach. "Argoran babies are very active during pregnancy."

Joni sniffed, still dealing with the wonder and novelty. They were having babies. "This is too cute."

More tears slid from Sylvie's blue eyes as she agreed. "It's beyond cute, Joni. We'll be moms together."

Arak nuzzled the side of Sylvie's blonde head, hands moving in a soothing motion over her belly. "Cute makes you both cry?"

Puzzlement and his cat's natural curiosity laced the question, causing them both to laugh. Sylvie tipped her head back and kissed Arak's cheek. He closed his eyes and purred, a distinct Argoran trait. Joni would deny the twinge of envy at the display if asked, but truthfully she thought it pretty fantastic that Sylvie had someone who loved her as openly as Arak did. The glib Jutak showered his mate in affection and public caresses. More so probably than Kyele, Torkel or Rydak together.

Joni pushed up to her feet and clapped her hands. "Well, you folks carry on with the sex and fun. I'm going to take the hover-car to the market place."

Arak stiffened and jerked his attention to Joni. "Kyele is leaving on a mission today, who are you taking with you?"

"Ever the protective soldier," Joni teased. "I'll have my knives."

His brows arched, damn him. "Joni, Torkel wants all of you to take protective measures when you leave the premises. After the last attack, you know it's not safe with the Marenians looking for an opportunity to strike back at the Jutak warriors."

Words of protest bubbled forth, but Sylvie shoved at Arak's arms, struggling to rise. "I'll go."

Arak tightened his hold and a low vibrating growl rolled forth. "You're staying here. Joni, ask Jaron to find someone to accompany you."

"Arak—"

"Kyele will kill me if he finds out I let you go alone." Then he added with a meaningful look, "Slowly. He'll kill all of us very, very slowly."

Sylvie's flushed face and tight lip reflected an imminent blowup, Joni backed off immediately not wanting to ruin their bonding time. "Fiiine. Only cause I love you guys." She winked and headed for the door. "I'll see if someone else is available."

Jaron was in the Communication center whirling through holo-screens, fingers flying over the ever-present data pad. He tapped the black bud in his ear and rattled off a bunch of codes and instructions she didn't understand. Joni waited until he flicked a glance in her direction.

His mouth twitched, but he waved her forward and she plopped into the chair beside him. When done, he rolled his chair to face her and shut down the holo screens of a shuttle taking off from Enotia. More than likely Kyele and his team.

"Should I be scared?" Jaron asked.

Shaking her head on a chuckle, Joni jumped right to the point. "I want to go to the market place and need someone to go with me. You interested?"

Jaron drummed his fingers on the desk. "That explains why Kyele insisted I run a scan on the remaining two hover-cars before he left."

Pleasure thumped Joni's chest hard. Her dark warrior loved her. Not in the vibrant way Arak did with kisses and hugs, not in the fierce protective way of Torkel. He was not as obvious. But this, this was exactly what she'd come to expect from him. Her safety and happiness was his main concern. He did things without her knowing yet she always benefited from the results.

"Does that mean yes?"

Jaron blew out a breath and rose. "Why not? You Earth women are always funny. You can teach me more of your world's sex terms."

For some reason, the Enotians thought this was extremely amusing, often asking Joni or the others to repeat a slang phrase or to explain in further detail while they tried to figure out how it made sense. Some things just didn't translate well.

"How soon?" She fluttered her lashes, hoping he'd be ready sooner than later.

Jaron snorted. "I'll take care of a few things here and comm Bane to cover."

Joni skipped to his side and looped an arm about his shoulders in a half-hug. "Thank you! Thank you! Thank you!"

Jaron patted her back awkwardly. "I could use the distraction. Just don't get me in trouble with Kyele by doing something crazy while we're there."

"Hmm." Joni pulled away and tapped a finger on her chin as if in deep thought.

"Earth women. Trouble."

Joni laughed, but she had no intention of doing anything wild. She wanted to shop and come back to her new home to wait for her Chosen. Her time as a sex slave with the Marenians was enough excitement to last a lifetime. She'd never jeopardize her happiness with Kyele by being reckless.

Chapter 4

Joni loved Enotia's market place. Alien vendors came from all over and the things available continued to boggle her mind. Beside her, Jaron stuffed his third fluffy pastry in his mouth. She had no idea where he put it on his lean frame. Casually dressed in black military pants and a tight black pullover shirt, there wasn't an inch of fat on him.

As she eyed unique bottles containing unimaginable scents, Jaron kept close and though he laughed at her jokes, his attractive features remained guarded. No one got in their way or hindered their stroll as a result. Or maybe it was the laser he wore belted at his waist and strapped down to his thigh. He didn't announce his status as a Jutak warrior, but the military bearing was easy to recognize.

For all his jovial attitude, Jaron was every bit the soldier Kyele and the others were. It was in his walk, the way he carried himself, shoulders upright and eyes constantly scanning the area.

"Joni!"

Jaron tensed, his hand going to his weapon. He dropped it immediately at the approach of the older blond couple. Shaya and Marlin. Behind them at a slower pace was Faye. Joni grinned and hugged each of them. They were Torkel's parents and wrapped everyone in a bubble of family. It helped a lot since she and her friends were so far from Earth.

Shaya moved from Joni's arms and straight to Jaron who she squeezed tight. Her head barely reached his chest and the tall Jutak had to bend slightly to accommodate her.

"How are you? Is my son taking care of everyone? Maybe I should send food."

Jaron escaped the hug, but a broad grin stretched his face when he pulled back. "Torkel is well."

Marlin wrapped an arm around his Chosen, drawing her back to his side. "We will visit tomorrow. Shaya is excited about the baby."

Shaya elbowed him and her nose scrunched. "We are *both* excited to have a new baby in the family."

Faye wisely remained quiet. Joni imagined she wouldn't hurt for a babysitter. Her heart twinged at the thought of how her own father and brother would react if she could share news of her pregnancy with them. Unfortunately the Singles Program she'd signed up for which sent her to the stars for a husband also mandated that participants eliminate contact with their past life.

"Well, there will be plenty of babies to love," Jaron added, with a side glance at her. "Joni will give birth after Faye and Sylvie."

Joni considered punching Jaron. They'd only discussed the pregnancy with Kyele's team members. Shaya's squeal eliminated the option. She smothered Joni in another hug. "This is wonderful news."

Shaya pulled back, hands gripping Joni's shoulders. Faye rolled her eyes and exchanged an amused glance with Joni. "How far? Has Dr. Maku shared the sex?"

Marlin's face suffused with pleasure as well. He patted Joni on the back awkwardly. All three stared, waiting for her answer. Joni gave in to her own bubbling excitement. "Only the early stages. Just under twelve weeks. It's a boy."

Shaya linked elbows with Joni on one side and Faye on the other. "Is that what brings you to the market place? Are you buying baby things?"

"Not yet." Joni loved shopping. Was addicted to it actually. "I'll see what catches my eye."

"Hmm. You can spend time with us. We'll talk babies, clothes and men."

Marlin made no effort to hide his groan. Jaron chuckled and stepped in line to follow as Shaya headed for the nearest stall. Shaya shooed Jaron. "You can leave, Jaron. Joni's safe with me. Tell my son I expect a visit soon."

Eyeing them with a hint of hope, Marlin asked, "Should I go too, my lovely Chosen?"

Shaya glared, her blue eyes darkening. "*You* are our escort. It's the only way Jaron won't feel obligated to stay, correct?"

When the attention shifted toward him, Jaron's cheeks tinged red. He bowed and winked at Shaya. "I believe you are in good hands with a former member of Enotia's government."

It had stunned Joni when she first learned Marlin Alonson had been a member of the Jutak warriors administration in his younger years. Torkel's papan had a gentle demeanor about him, reminding Joni of her own father with his strong core of honor and integrity. Apparently, there was a hidden side to the silver-haired sweetheart.

"Are you coming back with Joni, Faye?" Jaron asked.

She shook her head. "I'll have them drop me off later.

Jaron shifted his gaze to Joni. "You stay with the Alonsons. Do *not* separate. When it is time to go, the hover-car will be where we left it. I will contact Geile to take me back."

Knowing how serious the threat of danger was, Joni patted her ever-present knives on her thighs. "You don't have to worry, Jaron. When we're done here, I'll come straight back."

He cocked his head at her. Doubt flickered in his blue gaze. She could sense him wavering. "I should stay."

"Jaron," Joni drawled his name. "Trust me. I'm not flighty and I won't do anything to put myself in danger."

At that, he nodded and leaned forward to press a soft kiss to Joni's temple. His voice was whisper light when he spoke against her skin. "You are Kyele's everything. Have a care and stay safe."

A lump formed in Joni's throat because she knew no truer words were spoken. "What can happen between shopping and going home?"

She meant the question to be facetious, but Jaron stepped back and met her gaze intently. "Plenty. When you've been a soldier as long as me, you understand the easiest task can take a sudden turn."

An ominous shiver rolled down Joni's spine. The eerie sensation implied something bad was about to happen. Joni shook off the thought. Being pregnant was making her paranoid. Nothing bad was going to happen because her life was finally where she'd wanted it. And she was happy, damn it.

Jaron waved at Shaya and Marlin, offering another goodbye before leaving them. Shaya rubbed her hands together, glee shining from her gaze. "Where to start?"

***

"Kyele, closing in on your left."

Savi's warning had Kyele spinning on his heel in a crouch, firing his laser at the moving shadow. The target squeaked then stumbled. Kyele and Creed raced toward the fallen criminal.

"Jutak warriors!"

"Jutak warriors!"

The identifying call came up from all of them as they circled the individual. Creed did the honors and put the plasti-cuffs on the thick wrists of their target before rolling him over. Kyele kept his expression blank as he came face to face with the Chamele, a vicious criminal, who was responsible for the deaths of a dozen people.

Blood dripped from the laser burn on his thigh where he'd been hit. His skin flushed a bright red then a sickly green. "You didn't have to shoot me."

Stefin snorted and pulled Renard to his feet with a brutal grip on his forearm. Another squeak came out and Kyele grimaced. Running after being caught in the act of committing crimes ranked high as one of the stupidest things done when faced by Jutak warriors.

"You can't hurt me!"

Instead of responding to the complaint, Kyele pulled out his data pad, sent in the vid image proof of the arrest and commed a message to Jaron about the completion of the assignment.

His team members laughed and joked as they led Renard away. They'd be met by authorities at the air transport where custody would be transferred and the Chamele would be held until his sentencing to a prison colony for his deadly crimes.

Eagerness added an extra hitch to Kyele's stride. He hated being away from Joni now that she carried their child. He struggled with the fear and excitement of the coming birth. Watching Arak and Torkel, Kyele found himself thrilled like Arak yet terrified like Torkel.

Back on their shuttle, Markus glanced over at him. "You seem distracted, Kyele. Are you feeling sick?"

If Kyele hadn't been paying attention, he would have missed the glimmer of amusement in his teammate's eyes. Keeping his expression bland, he continued to stare and not respond. Markus shifted awkwardly in his seat while Creed and Savi laughed outright. Markus cleared his throat and developed a sudden interest in fixing his safety harness.

Reassured that he'd killed the possibility of his morning sickness being a future ongoing joke, Kyele leaned his head back against his seat and closed his eyes. Thoughts of Joni had him in a state of semi-arousal and anticipation. Would she wear one of the provocative outfits she loved to greet him in?

The seat next to him jostled and Kyele reluctantly banished visions of Joni and sex sharing.

Stefin had joined him. He met Kyele's gaze with a serious expression. "Everything good?"

The engines rumbled beneath them as the shuttle took off, taking them home to Enotian.

"I am fine," Kyele answered.

Stefin nodded. "Markus was joking. All of us are excited about you and your Chosen expecting a little one."

They were. Each time a teammate crossed the sands during presentation, the others showed their support by being there. There were no words for Kyele to express his gratitude for the men of Torkel's Unit who always stood by him and the dark moments he often had.

"Thank you, Stefin."

Another abrupt nod and Stefin leaned back to doze. Kyele liked that about his team as well. They laughed and joked, but also knew when to give him space. Like now. It wasn't as if Kyele didn't enjoy the camaraderie, he just preferred his own company sometimes. Unless it pertained to Joni.

If possible, he'd stay in her presence day in and day out. She filled a need he'd never known he had. As had becoming the Team Leader for Team Two. When Torkel offered the position to him as a sign of his faith in Kyele's leadership he'd been stunned. Slightly wary as well.

Kyele's heart lightened. He may have had an unlikely start in life with a path full of pain and scars, but it was all worth it to get where he was at this moment.

Joni made it worth it. And now they would have a baby. No one commented on the smile that curled his mouth for the remainder of the trip home.

Chapter 5

Joni kissed Shaya and Marlin goodbye before placing her single purchase in the hover-car. Much to her surprise, she'd only picked up a tiny white tee-shirt slightly bigger than her palm and trimmed in lace at the sleeves. It was her first baby item and despite her wish to wait until further along in the pregnancy, she'd gotten it because it was too adorable to walk away from. Faye had no such hesitation and had picked up dozens of baby outfits and blankets.

"Let Jaron know we took very good care of you," Shaya teased with a twinkle in her blue eyes as she and Marlin with Faye headed toward their own hover-car.

Joni chuckled and hopped into her seat behind the guiding wheel. The five-point harness slid into place the moment she touched the start button, cinching with a slight click. A few taps programmed the vehicle to return home. Gentle vibrations stirred beneath her. Joni navigated out of the lot with a final wave to Marlin and Shaya.

The ride back to the Jutak residence was an easy jaunt Joni had made on numerous occasions. Traffic tended to be light as Enotians traveled in groups or walked most places on their fancy automated sidewalks.

It completely caught Joni off-guard when something slammed into her on the passenger side. Her head snapped into the door frame. Joni cried out and glanced to the side.

Another hover-car had hit her. An image of a pale face, mouth open in a silent scream flashed then disappeared as metal ground against metal and the world spun. Another crash jerked her forward in her seat. Fire burned across her chest as the harness held her in place.

Joni's fingers accidentally hit the acceleration button, sending the hover-car zooming forward. The emergency wheels lowered and caught on a grooved part of the roadway. She gripped the steering guide, frantically pushing for the decel and brake button. Off balance, the hover-car rocked to the side, skidding several feet in the air then lurched.

Everything tipped over. Her head made contact again, this time with the window. The vehicle slammed down on all fours and Joni jolted in the harness.

"Kyele. Kyele. Kyele." She chanted his name under her breath like he was a genie capable of granting wishes. And she had a doozy of a wish. She remembered his long ago words when they spoke of her facing any future threats and took a deep breath.

"Stay calm, Joni." He smoothed locks of her red-gold hair back. "You're smart. All you have to do is hold on until I get to you."

He leaned in closer, his green eyes fever bright with promise. "I will come for you, Joni. Never doubt that my Chosen."

Trees loomed ahead on a direct collision course. Pain slammed through her body on contact. Joni blinked and the landscape changed as the angle of the vehicle tilted forward. Her heart banged against her chest. She knew this area. A cliff loomed ahead.

The drop off ended abruptly, an oasis of clear water below where Enotians often came to study rare birds that nested in the area.

This beautiful countryside was about to be her downfall. Joni braced for impact, feet pressed hard to the floor though there were no pedals. Her head jerked forward, sending her face smashing into the steering guide. Blood spurted, her nose crunched. The hover-car hit max speed and became airborne.

Joni screamed again. Branches smacked against the front window panel. A blunt force shoved her forward in her seat again. Joni raised her arms to protect her face.

The safety shielded window exploded with a boom. Her bare skin prickled as slices tore at her flesh. Burning pain ripped at the side of her neck. When the vehicle hit the ground again, the front end crumpled, shook, then the entire hover-car settled with a shudder.

'There has been a severe malfunction. Do you wish to report for assistance?'

The mechanical voice broke through Joni's panic and disorientation. She blinked, but something wet dripped down her face obscuring her vision. She tried to press the button for the emergency beacon, but her right arm flopped at her side.

'Failure to reply denotes automatic contact for authorities. Please do not leave the incident site until a report has been taken.'

"Kyele," Joni moaned as everything grayed and went hazy.

***

As soon as Team Two entered, Jaron directed Kyele to meet with Torkel in his office. Not an unusual request as his Unit Leader often wished to go over the details on a completed mission. The pleasure he felt at returning home vanished when Torkel rose from his seat at Kyele's entrance.

The downward curve of his mouth froze Kyele's heart mid-beat. Then it pulsed and banged against his chest at an unnatural rate.

"Have a seat, Kyele."

"Tell me," he countered.

Torkel's gaze darkened, sympathy and compassion glinting from his brown gaze. "There has been an accident."

Kyele eased one of the knives he always carried from his thigh sheath and started to twirl it between his fingers. Everything was fine. Joni was out buying things for their baby. He'd checked the hover-car before he left then had Jaron go over it as well. It was mechanically sound. None of the other men were around which meant the other Chosens were fine as well.

"Tell me." The words snapped out with more force the second time.

"I am sorry. It...is not good."

The blade clattered to the floor unnoticed. Had someone attempted to kidnap her again? Kyele's throat locked. He licked his suddenly dry lips and choked out the question. "Is she alive?"

Torkel hesitated and the small fissure in Kyele's chest spread into a jagged crack that sent him to his knees, fists braced on the floor. The ache rocked through his body until nothing penetrated. His eyes burned, but the tears would not fall. He gasped, unable to draw air into his lungs. Not Joni. Not his *tesa*.

Pain struck as Kyele tried to wrap his mind around what Torkel didn't say. How was he to move on without Joni in his life?

"Kyele! Kyele, I sent Dr. Maku ahead to stabilize Joni because we couldn't risk moving her. We have to hurry if you are to say goodbye."

Kyele blinked and looked up at his Unit Leader. Goodbye? His brain stuttered. Confusion caused his voice to go hoarse. "What?"

"We need to get you to Joni."

"Where?" Would he have to view her beautiful face in death to end this nightmare?

Torkel placed a hand on his shoulder. "Not far from the market square. There was an accident. Medics are on scene."

He stumbled to his feet. Torkel's words gave him hope. "She is not dead?"

"No, but—"

Kyele didn't wait to hear more. He misted into his Spectar form, traveling faster than he ever had before to get to his Chosen's side, all the while begging, pleading and bargaining with any entity listening. And in the end, he begged the one who mattered most. The one who'd promised not to let the darkness take him. "I'm coming, Joni. Hold on for me."

When Kyele arrived at the site, medics and their assistants crowded around an upside down hover-car. Beside it, two men followed a sheet covered hoverboard. Kyele's heart tumbled to his stomach. He pressed a fist to his chest as he approached with staggering steps. He parted his lips to speak, but words froze. Nothing came out.

"Jutak warrior Bastien?" The blond on the left asked.

Kyele could only nod, his eyes burning with unshed tears.

"Dr. Maku said to direct you to the second vehicle below."

Kyele glanced at the body. If Maku wasn't here then this wasn't Joni. Relief splintered inside of him, but he had no time to waste and raced off to find Joni.

The scene below was worse than the one above. This second hover-car was totaled, the wreck almost unrecognizable for the damage that had been done. Gouges left jagged tears in the ground from the top of the hill to the bottom. Trees had been ripped from their roots and leaned heavily to the side, their trunks split into wooden spears. Imagining the event which could cause such devastation was a nightmare Kyele didn't want to contemplate Joni experiencing.

Dr. Maku knelt next to another blanket covered body on the ground and waved him over. Several medical professionals in their distinctive blue uniforms surrounded Maku. Kyele hurried forward and jerked to a halt when he spotted familiar bright red-gold hair. Joni. He choked and fell to his knees beside her. Her head tipped to the side, facing in his direction.

Strict training kept him from reacting outwardly to her appearance while inside his heart shattered. One golden eye was swollen shut and the surrounding area was colored a vivid purple and red. Abrasions marred her cheeks in violet streaks puckered at the end as if something tore across it. He swallowed back bile at seeing her hurt like this.

"Hey," she whispered. Blood smeared her entire face in ghastly trails, a thin line trickling from her mouth and still, she found the strength to smile.

It took two tries for Kyele to get the harshly rasped word past his dry lips. "Hey."

"She needs to be treated. Transferred to a med center," Maku murmured, expression more grave than Kyele had ever witnessed.

One of the health workers shook his head, regret shining from his gaze. Kyele's soul shuddered but he forced himself to lock down the fear threatening to overtake him. Turning from the worker, he eased back the chest high blanket covering Joni.

Nothing. He sat back on his haunches with a huff. He expected the worst. Instead there was nothing. No catastrophic injuries to explain the palpable air of horror and grief. She wore the same midriff baring top from earlier, her tanned torso smooth and clear.

The barely noticeable curve to her belly reminded him of their child. Kyele gingerly placed his palm there.

Suddenly, Joni coughed, her body arching in on itself. The movement left her whimpering, her distress flaying the flesh from Kyele's bones. Maku called out medical terms and jargon to the others as he gently guided her flat on her back again. Someone slapped an injector in Maku's hand and he depressed the plunger against Joni's forearm. She gasped, paling further until her skin took on a chalky cast.

Panic hit Kyele. "What is wrong with her?"

Someone else moved the swath of hair from her neck. Just a slight adjustment to the matted red waves and gorge rose in Kyele's throat. He couldn't take his eyes from the morbid sight. A large piece of metal pierced the side of her slim throat, bright red blood splattered around the entry.

Joni mumbled something he missed. Kyele leaned close to her face to better hear. "What?"

"I love you," she whispered.

He kissed the lone tear as it slid down her cheek. "As I love you."

"I held on," Joni murmured. "Just like you said to do in an emergency."

He smiled, but the sides quivered. Then he pressed his lips tight. "And I came for you. Always."

The lines on her forehead smoothed out. She arched a patent Joni brow full of cockiness. Except blood caked her brows from gashes on her forehead where projectiles had sliced at her delicate skin. "I was the best Chosen."

Kyele kissed the side of her mouth. Whisper soft. "You *are* the best Chosen for me. No other will own a place in my heart."

The rise of her chest slowed. Her breath caught and blood bubbled from her lips with her next words. "We were damn good together, Ky."

He nodded, taking a moment to speak beyond the growing lump in his throat. She kept referencing them in the past tense. Kyele had no intention of giving up on them. "Do you trust me?"

"I've always trusted you, Ky."

Truth. She'd trusted him from the moment they met and never lost faith when he resisted the inevitable.

"Close your eyes, Joni. I've got you."

"What are you doing, Kyele?" Maku looked concerned as Kyele shifted and crouched over Joni. He braced his arms at the sides of her head, careful not to touch the metal.

The minute her lashes fluttered closed, Kyele shifted to his Spectar form and allowed himself to flow into Joni. It was easy to destroy an enemy from within using his birthright. Only once before had Kyele used his abilities for a different reason.

Like then, he merged himself with Joni in an attempt to save her life.

His body seamlessly joined with hers. They became one, his Spectra form able to discern more like this. There was no other way to explain it. With the joining, he could identify...wrongness.

Kyele let his gift guide him and his attention focused on the beacon of light at the core of Joni. Alive. She was alive and he fucking planned for her to stay that way.

Drums sounded in the distance, each thump discordant. Fast, fast then double tap before resuming the manic pace. Disoriented, he hesitated in the thick darkness, unable to tell which way to go or what to do.

Focusing all of his senses, Kyele drew closer to the large object pulling his attention. Joni's heart. It lost its cadence and Kyele's essence swirled around it in panic. Something warned him not to touch the precious organ though. Kyele turned his gaze elsewhere.

The swish of water filled his ears. Kyele's incorporeal form hovered, Joni's life force all around him wavering as if her body would quit at any moment.

So many injuries. All of it tugging on him to heal everything at once but he couldn't.

Anger surged through his veins along with fear. Focus. He needed to find the fatal injury site at her neck and fix it first. With that thought in mind, he searched the endless black around him, seeking to find the right path. If he couldn't save his Chosen, the reason he woke each morning, then he might as well give up.

Please. Please, don't leave me, Joni.

Something brushed against him. A warmth he didn't usually sense without his corporal body. The heat formed a pattern and with time pressing on him, Kyele followed the stream to the source. As he drew closer, the heat became a blazing fire around a central point.

Flinching, Kyele reached forward and surrounded the coiled knot. This, this was the source of the pain and the death reaper seeking to take Joni. He touched it with a firm grasp, intending to physically hold her to this plane if he had to. Kyele pushed with everything he had until the knot was out.

Lightning crackled in an arc, blinding his senses. Kyele fought back with a blast of energy. There was only one thought on his mind.

Save Joni. Nothing else mattered. He flowed deeper into the burning circle, increasing the merge until he became one with the fire hot hole left behind at the mass' center. There were loose strands of red, white and black swirling everywhere. Kyele made frantic grabs for each, hoping to find a means of reattaching them wherever they belonged.

Please, he begged. *I need you, Joni.*

Each time he stretched the strands back to the knot, they stayed so he worked faster until no loose piece flowed freely. Upon completion, he hovered, trying to decipher if there was something more he could do. Stars exploded followed by a wave of black, throwing Kyele back. He roared in denial. His physical body tugged at his Spectar form, drawing him away.

No! Not yet. He wasn't done. He needed to be sure.

"Kyele!" Maku yelled.

Kyele jerked, his eyes opening to the night sky above. *Joni!* He rolled over to his side on a groan. "W-w-what happened?"

Maku swiped his eyes on the shoulder of his shirt. His hands busily worked. "I don't know what you did. It...you...I'm never going to assume anything when dealing with you, Jutaks."

Kyele pushed up. He was on the ground beside Joni. Her eyes were closed. She was still. So still. He stretched his hand toward her face. She sighed, breath stirring his palm before he cupped her jaw. Maku slapped a pressure bandage to the side of her neck.

Kyele's heart jumped. "Will she live?"

Maku waved the medics away and lowered his voice. He nodded at the discarded piece of metal to the side on the ground. "Whatever you did worked. It pushed from her skin on its own. I have never seen such. I was able to get the bleeding stopped and gave her a sedative in addition to the pain inhibitor. Once we get back home, I can take care of the other minor wounds with the neutralizer."

Home. Joni alive was all Kyele wanted.

Chapter 6

Joni awoke with a groan and stretched. The bed beneath her was hard. Frowning, she opened her eyes and glanced around the all white room. This wasn't home. Her heart fluttered as she shoved up to a seated position.

"Wait, *tesa*." A firm hand pushed on her shoulder.

She'd know that husky voice anywhere. "Kyele? Why am I in the medic center?"

Dark hair messy and green eyes drawn, he pulled his chair closer to the bed she rested on. "You had an accident. In the hover-car."

It all came back and Joni pressed a palm to her middle. "Our baby?"

Kyele placed his hand over hers. "Safe. He is fine. As are you."

Joni dropped back on the bed with a relieved huff. "The other vehicle...it just appeared. I was driving safely."

Kyele squeezed her hand. "No one holds you at fault. The other driver died, but investigation shows mechanical failure. It caused her hover-car to slam into yours. The collision pushed you over the cliff."

Hearing it relayed in such a blunt manner sent Joni's heart racing. That easily she could have lost all she held dear. A wet trickle tickled her cheek. Another followed. The chair squeaked and Kyele rose to join her in the tight, narrow bed. His muscled arms pulled her close until she nestled against his strong chest.

Joni sniffled trying to draw on his strength. Kyele lowered his head to the top of hers and nuzzled her hair. "Do not cry. It hurts my heart."

"I knew you'd come for us." Her first and last thought were of Kyele and those kept her from being as scared as she could have been. Forcing back more tears, Joni leaned back and smiled. "The day you and Arak rescued us is the best thing to ever happen to me. All I went through doesn't compare to the good I have in my life now. I wouldn't change a thing because it's made me who I am."

***

As Kyele lay behind her on his side, he contemplated her words. With care in every move, he trailed a finger down the outside of Joni's arm, flesh pebbling in the wake. Wonder, joy, emotions he couldn't put into words filled him. Would his amazement ever get old? Again he brushed his fingertips over her. From collarbone down to her midsection he stroked ever so gently.

"I love who you are." It was getting easier and easier to say the words casually though there was nothing casual about his feelings. Kyele closed his eyes on an exhale and moved his hold to Joni's waist. Nice and light, when he really wanted to squeeze her and hold on so that nothing could take her from him.

"I see our patient is up."

Joni jerked in his arms as Dr. Maku entered the room. He stopped next to the bed and though he frowned at Kyele, he didn't comment on his presence beside Joni.

"Is everything really alright with the baby?" she asked breathlessly.

Maku nodded and handed over his data pad. Kyele tipped his head down to see as well. On screen, they viewed the outline of a tiny form curled and hunched over.

"This is the recording I made as soon as we brought you in. Your son is thriving and measuring on track when I compare him to Sylvie and Faye's records."

Another worry dispelled. Kyele rubbed his hand over Joni's belly bared by the shift in her position to accept the data pad from Maku. She traced her finger over the white outline on the screen. "He's so tiny."

Kyele studied the small arms, bent knees and unusually large head. He was deciding on whether to question the size when the image blurred. Joni squeaked and twitched in his arms. Kyele caught her before she rolled from the bed to the floor.

"What happened?"

Maku leaned over to see where Joni pointed on the screen and a bemused smile creased his cheeks. "Yes. That is different from the others, but more due to your Chosen's heritage than any problem with your pregnancy."

Kyele frowned until it hit him what had occurred. He chuckled and kissed the side of Joni's face. "His Spectar form."

Even as he said it, the hunched body of their child reappeared on the screen. Maku pointed to a column of numbers on the side. "If you watch closely you will note the stats never fade when he does that. The scan is monitoring his vitals continuously. Like I said this was taken earlier. I can get a connector and show you real time."

Joni shook her head and gave Maku the data pad back. She settled in the bed. "As long as he's fine, I won't worry."

Kyele caressed the small bump of her belly. "My little Earthling."

She cupped his jaw. "The rest of this pregnancy will go smoothly. You'll see."

Kyele would hold fervent hope that she was right. His heart could only take so much.

Author Note

I have to say that some characters become a favorite of mine the moment they show up on page. Kyele and Joni are such characters. It is a joy any time I get to revisit them or share an intimate moment of their relationship. Sometimes, I even learn something myself.

If you're new to A World Beyond and interested in their HEA, their full story can be found in Kyele's Passion. You'll also get to see their son and more information about Kyele's parents and the heritage he references in their book.

Michelle H.

Moment in Time

A World Beyond Novella

By Michelle Howard

Published by MH Publications

Chapter 1

The hum of activity and conversation echoed in the two-story lobby of the exhibition building. In a celebration acknowledging the birth of the Enotian military force and elite soldiers, the government facilities at this particular location were open to the public.

Laughter and smiles graced the faces of every visitor. It was a good sight. A happy one, considering the recent turmoil with the inhabitants of Marenia starting to expand the slave trade beyond their own home world

"Did you ever think we would be this lucky?"

The gentle voice disturbed his musings. Marlin grinned and leaned down to rub his jaw over the top of his Chosen's soft blonde hair. "I was lucky the day you chose me."

Shaya melted against him with a heartfelt sigh, her arms going around his waist in an embrace as familiar as her scent. She loved with her whole heart and Marlin never imagined someone like her wanting to spend her life with him. Especially after he'd disclosed the low likelihood of ever being able to have children due to a genetic anomaly discovered during a childhood examination.

That hadn't mattered at all to Shaya and she'd walked directly toward him during presentation, the ceremony to legalize relationships, and offered to spend her life by his side.

"We are both fortunate then." She leaned away and smiled at him.

Marlin brushed back strands of golden blonde hair, smoothing pieces behind her ears. "We share a son and a daughter. Our family is complete in a way I never expected."

Shaya stretched and pecked his chin with a loud, smacking kiss. "I knew the moment I saw you on the sands, we'd live a dream-filled life. Even if children were not a possibility."

Unlike some who walked the sands of presentation looking for a lifelong partner, Marlin hadn't known Shaya. They'd accidently met while he'd been out with a friend one day. They'd spoken of light-hearted things, including their mutual participation in the upcoming presentation ceremony. Then she'd smiled as she went on her way with a group of women.

It took a leap of faith to form a bond with only a few lines of history about another but becoming a Chosen through the process on their home world was a time honored tradition which produced many successful relationships.

His friend, Taig, had elbowed him in the side that day and declared, "She will be my Chosen. Mark my words."

Marlin had no answer because there had been a undeniable current running through him when he'd touched Shaya's arm. Desire and an incredible need had also burst through his chest.

After a firm squeeze, Marlin let his arms slide away from her trim waist and glanced to the side. Chattering in low voices, their two children stood side by side studying the display case with holo images of the first Jutak warrior unit. One dark head and one blonde.

As if sensing his stare, their son turned. At twelve years of age, he still hadn't lost his enthusiasm and hope. Brown eyes met Marlin's, his gaze solemn yet bright with suppressed excitement.

They didn't share a drop of blood between them. Torkel was of Marenian descent, a ruthless race with nefarious connections to every conceivable evil, but Marlin couldn't love him more. The day the abandoned baby appeared on the farm where they lived ranked as one of his greatest memories.

Or maybe that honor was reserved for the day his Chosen defied the birth center and kidnapped the unclaimed baby. A smile of remembrance creased Marlin's face. A good day indeed because he'd become a proud papan that day. After he prevented Shaya from being arrested of course.

"I know that look."

Marlin snorted and faced Shaya. "What look?"

She poked his mid-section. "You are thinking of the day we brought Torkel into our hearts."

Their daughter, Lissi, tugged on her brother's hand pulling him to the next display and successfully drawing Torkel's focus from Marlin. There were times, not many, but a few when Marlin caught flickers of doubt and fear from their son. He wasn't sure what was causing his new signs of distress and planned to wait before mentioning it to Shaya and putting her overprotective attentions on Torkel.

"Look, Tor!"

Tiny and delicate in comparison, Lissi had the looks of an Enotian. Unlike Torkel's golden skin tones and dark coloring, she was blonde with blue eyes.

Her conception came as a complete and welcome surprise years after they'd adjusted to having a son to cherish. Marlin had known at an early age that his future might not include children yet here he was with not one but two.

Looping an arm around Shaya's waist, he grinned. "Actually, I was thinking of how I received a call that my Chosen was about to be sent to a prison colony for abducting a child."

Shaya's full-throated chuckle burst forth, drawing Torkel's attention once more. She laughed until tears sparkled on her eyelids and Marlin couldn't resist planting another kiss on her flushed cheeks.

Not a drop of remorse reflected in her smug blue gaze, but her tone was dead serious. "A maman will risk anything for her child."

Something she'd made very clear to those working at the center where they'd taken Torkel in case his Marenian birth parents came back for him.

"It is a story I plan to tell Torkel when he is old enough," Marlin added.

Her smile lingered, eyes lit with curiosity. "You do not think he will be hurt that none wanted him?"

Marlin ran a hand down her back and left it braced above the full curve of her butt. "I think he will feel enormously grateful that someone, *you*, loved him enough to risk your freedom."

While it was the truth as he saw it, Shaya relaxed against him with a sigh as if she'd needed the verbal confirmation. "We will tell him together."

Marlin lifted his free hand. "Torkel, Lissi, it is time to move on to the upper level. The Jutak warriors have prepared a special training demo."

Torkel's mouth fell open as he and Lissi ran over to join them. His son loved hearing about Marlin's administration job with the government military force and spent most of his time at home asking Marlin non-stop questions.

"Remember," Marlin counseled. "Follow the rules and the day will go without a hitch."

***

"Yes, papan," Torkel recited, barely able to contain his enthusiasm.

Beside him, Lissi bounced on her toes and grinned. "Yes, papan."

His maman and papan groaned at the innocent tone. With her blonde ringlets and bright blue eyes, his sister appeared sweet. And she was. Most times.

Looking at her, no one would believe she hid his favorite toys and put fruit jellies in his hair while he slept. Papan said she liked making mischief. Torkel agreed with him. Maman sent Lissi to the gardens for lots of reflection time, but Torkel wasn't sure it worked because she always found new trouble.

Uniformed guards arrived and spoke with his parents. In a low voice, Torkel murmured, "You need to be good today, Lis."

Her mouth pursed and her lashes fluttered. "I will be *very* good, Tor."

He grimaced. She never managed to say his name right and he'd given up trying to teach her. "Please, Lis."

She reached out and entwined chubby fingers with his own. "Promise."

She made the vow in a solemn voice and Torkel gave in to the urge to tug her close and hug her. Her hair smelled like his maman's flowers because she'd had reflection time again before they left. He couldn't stay mad at his sister. When she was born, he gave a silent oath to always protect the tiny baby who joined their family. He always would.

Chapter 2

Torkel was riveted by every part of the presentation. The public viewing was over and soon guests would be asked to leave the large conference room. Beside him, his sister leaned her head on the arm he had propped on the chair between them, her eyes heavy-lidded and drowsy. Lissi hadn't been quite as enthralled as him. Or perhaps it was that she was too young to fully appreciate all they'd seen.

"I need to use the cleansing room to touch up my enhancements. Wait for me here," his maman murmured to his papan as she rose from her seat.

His papan stood, kissed his maman's hand then stared at her retreating back as she made her way down the aisle and disappeared through the arched doorway. Respect and admiration colored the interactions of all those who stopped and spoke to Marlon Alonson while they waited. His papan was the epitome of everything Torkel wanted to be when he grew up.

His chest clenched as he remembered the thoughts plaguing his mind of late. Maybe *he* wasn't deserving of such respect. Marenians were not admired and Torkel was Marenian. By blood anyway. In his mind and heart he was Enotian.

"Papan!"

Lissi popped up from her semi-nap and skipped down the row toward their papan. A few feet away, she leaped into the air, secure and confident as always that she'd be caught. Those close by turned and stared as Lissi squealed when their papan lifted her high then settled her on his broad shoulders to sit. Her tiny legs draped his papan's neck.

"What did you think, Torkel?" his papan asked as he approached.

Pushing away his dark feelings about his birth heritage, Torkel straightened and locked his hands behind his waist as he'd seen the Jutak warriors do. "It was perf—"

Sudden screams split the air before cutting off abruptly. Torkel jumped. The crowd turned as one, confusion flashing across their faces. The *zip zip* of laser blasts followed. Torkel only recognized the sound because his papan had allowed him to view a holo-vid on a weapons demonstration just weeks ago.

Concern darkened his papan's face. He swiveled Lissi from his shoulders and to the floor in a blink then shoved her in Torkel's direction. "Grab your sister's hand!"

Tiny fingers grasped his in a death grip before Torkel could reach for Lissi. She trembled so hard her little body bumped against his side in a steady beat. More screams ripped through the room and the crowd began to run en masse.

A vise squeezed Torkel's chest as he looked to the man he admired for direction. For the first time in his life, Torkel was afraid. "Papan?"

Marlin had a hand at his shoulder, nudging gently, but firmly. "Move, son! Go!"

Torkel hurried along the row until he hit the aisle. Another nudge and he quickened his pace up toward one of the only three exits. Everyone had the same idea.

There were too many bodies pressing forward. The stench of terror saturated the air with its sour odor. Streams of people flowed by, racing ahead. Sweat formed on Torkel's brow and he laced his fingers tighter with Lissi, afraid she would be torn away. A quick glance down revealed tears falling down her cheeks though she didn't utter a sound. That alone would have worried Torkel. His sister didn't know the meaning of quiet.

His papan leaned down and brushed a reassuring hand over Torkel's head. He spoke in a rushed whisper. "We will get out of here. Stay calm."

Each doorway became jammed with dozens of bodies trying to force their way through all at once. Torkel was far from calm but decided to follow his papan's lead. He breathed deeply and continued moving. Shoving ensued from behind and he slipped with a sharp cry. The thought of being trampled locked his throat.

"Torkel!" Lissi screamed as her fingers slid from his.

The momentum flung him forward despite his effort to cling to his sister. Something banged his elbow and his hip smashed into a chair to the left. His papan caught his arm, but Torkel fought to break away and searched under the seats. He saw Lissi and yanked his sister back toward him. This time he clamped an arm about her waist and hugged her close.

"Good job, Torkel," his papan murmured as they reached the doorway on a huge surge and burst through.

Panic reigned. It was hard to focus in the confusion with people swelling around them, but his papan ignored it all to drop to one knee beside him and Lissi with a hard stare. He cupped them each on the shoulder. "I need you both to listen carefully. Do you remember where my office is?"

They both nodded. His papan chucked them under the chin and managed a grin. "Good. Torkel, take your sister there and lock the door."

Lissi sobbed and wrapped her arms around his neck. Torkel wanted to join her, but he put on a brave front and held in his own cries. He didn't need his papan's strained features to know this was serious.

His papan patted Lissi's back and quieted her down. When he pulled away, he wiped at her tears with a shaky thumb. "Be brave for papan, hmm? Torkel will take care of you. I must get to your maman."

And just like that, Torkel's heart dropped, stomach knotted into a ball. His maman had left before the shooting started. Where was she? What if she was hurt and needed them?

Papan stood and an expression Torkel had never seen crossed his face. Stern. Forceful. "I will come for you after. Run now!"

Torkel hesitated, uncertain if he wanted to leave either of his parents. His papan met his gaze and gave him a solid nod. The trust in his blue eyes was all Torkel needed. "Yes, papan."

Torkel took off running, dragging Lissi in his wake. They tore through the crowd, dodging bodies and everyone looking for a way out. Running against the tide wasn't easy, but Torkel had no intentions of failing. His papan expected him to take care of his sister and he would.

***

For the thousandth time in her life, Shaya contemplated using cosmetic enhancements. She leaned across the basin in the cleansing room and stared at her reflection in the mirror. Did Marlin want her to add more lip color and something to make her eyes stand out? Did he like her cheeks with a hint of rosy color?

As quickly as the thoughts occurred, Shaya dismissed it. Her Chosen was nothing if not honest and straight forward. He didn't care how she looked only that she loved him. And she did. Shaya loved Marlin with all her heart and the same intensity of the first time they'd met on the sands of presentation.

Hidden behind his civil veneer was an untamed wildness. Every step confident and steady, she had made her way across the glittering sand to make Marlin her Chosen and she'd do it again and again to have him in her life.

With a huff, Shaya turned from her reflection. What she'd applied earlier before leaving home was sufficient. She stuffed the colorful tubes back into a small decorative bag she'd brought with her then washed her hands. Others entered behind her and after exchanging polite smiles, Shaya gathered her bag and left.

Perhaps on the way home, they'd take the kids to eat at Santagos. Nothing gave Shaya more pleasure than being out with her family. Smiling, she headed toward the hall on the left, anxious to return.

Two men in dark clothing burst past her with fierce frowns pinching their brows. She paused to consider who or what had caused their frantic pace when the lights flickered. Someone gasped and Shaya hurried toward the stairs leading to the upper auditorium. She'd prefer to be with Marlin soothing their kids if the power went out.

Within a few feet from the turn she needed to take, a loud boom sounded. Lasers fired and Shaya came to an abrupt stop.

Somewhere behind her a woman screamed. Shaya turned to see what was happening and was bumped roughly by fleeing guests.

"Everyone on the ground! Now! Now!"

Ignoring the shouted command, a man darted around Shaya and the fizz of lasers sounded again. He dropped to the floor beside her, body limp. Hand to her throat, she half-stepped backward and stumbled. She barely muffled her gasp.

"Drop, drop! No one move!"

Regaining her footing, Shaya glanced up in the direction of the barked orders. Her blood froze. Coming from another section of the building, a group of four armored clad men with darkened helmets over their heads marched down the hall.

"You! Get over there with the others."

Shaya jerked and realized one of the armed men was pointing at her with a blunt gloved finger. Heart jumping, she took a deep breath and moved in the direction he instructed. "Do not hurt anyone. It will only make things worse."

If she could calm them down, it would give their military force and the elite Jutak warriors time to act.

"No talking!" he screamed.

The crowd gathered against the wall grew as more and more of those attending were rounded up. Shaya stood to the right of a crying woman being held by her Chosen, head tucked beneath his clenched jaw. On her left, two little ones hid behind their parents' knees, eyes wide and faces pale as a sheet.

Her pulse skipped a beat as she thought of her own family. As quick as the worry occurred, she relaxed. Marlin would see to their children and make sure nothing happened to them.

With that in mind, Shaya eyed the men yelling and shoving people about until they seemed satisfied. She eased into a corner, enough to see but not be seen. They'd amassed a large group, but not as many as who had attended today's event. Maybe the others had managed to get out or were hiding.

"Listen carefully." The leader moved to the front and ripped the helmet from his head with one hand while holding his automated laser casually at his side.

The first thing Shaya noticed was his dark red hair and deep green eyes. Those were not the looks of a true Enotian. Their race was predominantly blond and blue eyed.

"I am Jordan. No one needs to get hurt unless they resist." He glared at a particular vocal man being held back by a woman's grip on his elbow. They both settled after a pointed moment of silence. "We are looking for the Prime Minister scheduled to speak here today."

The assumed leader walked back and forth in front of them. At his words, Shaya eased behind the bulk of a government employee dressed in a light gray uniform. Due to Marlin's career in the Enotian government, he was good friends with several prominent officials, namely Prime Minister Revin.

"Talk," he snarled. "We wish only to talk. No harm intended."

The silence in response to his question continued aside from the occasional sniffle or cry. His green eyes darkened and the tension in the atmosphere increased. One of his armed associates came to his side. Jordan tipped his head to the floor, listening to the whispered information.

When he lifted his head, Shaya barely managed to contain a gasp at the rage flashing across his attractive features.

"It would seem, the Prime Minister has left." He stalked forward, glaring at each person his eyes made contact with. "Let us see if we can get him on the communicator. Perhaps he will wish to talk when he realizes we will not be releasing his precious citizens until our demands are met."

Another two intruders stormed into their alcove, pushing and shoving a trembling group of young women. The men she'd witnessed rushing by. "Get with the others!"

They stumbled and cried out, but raced to join the knot of people. Shaya understood their relief. It was natural to hope there was safety in numbers.

Jordan stopped in front of a portly man in the familiar gray uniform of a government employee. Shaya recognized him since he'd greeted her and Marlin upon their arrival and given them special seating because he knew how much Torkel was interested in the Jutaks. "You! Come here."

Tak straightened his shoulders and moved forward with crisp steps. Jordan grabbed him by the collar of his jacket and pulled him off balance the rest of the way. Several people gasped.

Jordan clenched his fingers in the fabric and tugged again, forcing Tak down to his knees. Despite the rough handling, not once did Tak flinch or make a sound. The only visible sign of Tak's anger was his narrowed-eyed stare.

Jordan leaned over him, pressing the muzzle of his laser to Tak's temple and tapped. A cruel grin twisted Jordan's lips. "How do you contact your Prime Minister?"

Tak remained tight lipped.

"I. Said. How. Do. You. Contact. Him?" With each word, Jordan pressed the tip of the laser into the side of Tak's head.

Shaya could see the red crease from where she stood. "If you don't answer, I will have my men start shooting."

In spite of the weapon aimed right at his head, Tak shoved to his feet and gritted out, "The communicators."

Satisfaction gleamed as Jordan smiled and waved the barrel of the laser toward the crowd. "Get back with the others."

Tak tugged at his crumpled uniform jacket and joined them. Shaya breathed a sigh of relief, carefully watching as a communicator was ordered to be found. Jordan spun around to face them. "Everyone in the room over there."

Shaya glanced behind them and one of the guards opened the door to the mini-ballroom that was used for charity functions. Along with everyone else, she was herded from the hall and into the larger space.

There had to be over fifty guests with her. She remembered her surprise at the exclusive guest list containing over a hundred names. That meant half of the people visiting had either left earlier or escaped when chaos erupted.

As soon as the last person entered, the door was locked. Shaya inhaled sharply, fear tickling at her senses. The ballroom was empty of any significant furniture, a few round tables turned sideways and propped along the wall. A rack of chairs on a green skid had been left in a corner. The shiny tiled floors mocked with its brilliant sheen from an enthusiastic cleaner and the soaring ceiling added to the vast feeling.

"Stay calm," Jordan spoke with a smirk as a communicator was handed to him. "If your Prime Minister is as earnest as he claims, this will all be over soon."

He fiddled with the device for a few moments then cursed under his breath. "I need the Prime Minister's comm code."

Once more no one volunteered the information.

"I'm very tired of playing." Without further warning, Jordan shot at the woman who'd been clinging to her Chosen.

She screamed and grabbed at her calf. Her Chosen dropped beside her, both their hands pressing down on the bleeding wound. They were so young, tears streaming down both their faces.

Without pausing Jordan aimed at another and fired. The victim clutched his arm and fell against the wall behind him. The color leached from his face as he clasped his injured forearm. It was more than Shaya could take. She pushed beyond a few bodies to get in front of the row of shuddering people. "Enough! You said no one would get hurt."

Jordan eyed her speculatively and lowered his weapon. "Do you have the comm code I seek?"

Shaya nodded and recited the code that would give him direct access. It was a small thing to reveal to prevent him from injuring any others because no matter what Jordan said, it was clear they were all at risk regardless of how his conversation with the Prime Minister went.

While he placed the call, Shaya made a fervent wish. *Please, love, take care of our children if I don't make it.*

Chapter 3

After seeing Torkel and Lissi head in the general direction of his office, Marlin stopped an employee rushing by. "What's going on?"

The red-faced young woman spoke in a rapid whisper, throwing glances over her shoulder all the while. "Armed intruders. Get out before they catch you too."

She darted away before Marlin could question her further. "Alonson."

Marlin turned at the call. Striding toward him with determined steps and dressed entirely in an intimidating black uniform was one of his closest friends. It had been almost a year since they last connected. "It's good to see you, Taig."

They embraced and clapped one another on the back. Taig Vorik stepped away first, his blue eyes piercing Marlin with an intense stare. "I knew you were on site. Hoped to the stars you'd made it out. Where is your family?"

Marlin shook his head. "We were still in the room for the Jutak warriors' presentation when they struck. I sent Torkel and Lissi ahead to hide in my office."

Taig gripped the back of his neck with one hand and dropped the other to his hip and the laser holstered there. "What of Shaya?"

Marlin pretended to not hear how his friend's tone softened on his Chosen's name. There was no room for concern because Shaya had walked the sands toward him, not Taig. "Missing. She went to the cleansing room on the lower level before the attack occurred. I'm on my way to search for her."

Fear flashed in Taig's gaze, gone in an instant. "The benefit of the demonstration being held here is that there is a full Jutak team on premise. We'll find her."

It was what Marlin had to cling to. Shaya was smart. Brilliant. If trapped inside, he had utmost faith his Chosen *would* find a way to survive. Not *if*. Marlin bit back a sigh. No way would Shaya leave him and their children. She was somewhere in this building. He only hoped he managed to find her before anything happened.

Taig tapped the discreet black bud in his ear and waved his fingers for Marlin to follow as he turned away. "Vorik, here. Check in."

Unable to hear the Jutak's on the other end of the conversation, Marlin kept pace as they hurried down the carpeted hall. He ignored the artifacts on display which had held Lissi's attention, ignored the abandoned feel on this floor and ruthlessly crushed the terror trying to take hold of him.

"Approaching your location now." Taig faced Marlin as they neared a closed door. "My team's on the other side."

Marlin didn't allow himself to feel relief. That wouldn't happen until he had his family safe and at home. They entered the room which wasn't much bigger than a storage area. There were boxed supplies crammed in a corner with miscellaneous racks stacked on top. A few he recognized as cleaning material.

His gaze landed on the other occupants. Four soldiers with black masks pushed up on their heads waited. Blond hair disheveled, they stood upright, gazes burning. Dressed in black from head to toe, each wore a deadly knife strapped on one thigh and a hand-held laser strapped on the other.

"This is a good friend of mine, Marlin Alonson."

The men eyed him carefully then nodded.

"Give me a report," Taig demanded.

"Six armed intruders invaded the center on the main floor of the hall using force and smoke bombs directly following the event. During the confusion, they seem to have taken many of the guests hostage."

Marlin froze, listening intently as they exchanged details and the sparse amount of information they'd gathered. Taig clenched his jaw during the recital, closing his eyes at one point and muttering a curse.

While they discussed solutions and probable countermeasures, Marlin fought the need to act without caution. It wasn't easy when part of him wanted to rush out and find Shaya. He surveyed the room they were in again. With six fairly large men in the space, it was close quarters.

"Marlin, my team and I will do recon and return here with a status," Taig said as he redirected his attention toward him.

Shaking his head, Marlin rejected the idea instantly. To the depths of his soul, if someone harmed Shaya, he wouldn't be able to restrain himself. "No. I'm not leaving Shaya alone out there."

Taig's lips firmed. "She won't be alone. There are dozens of people being held with her."

Marlin remained silent refusing to comply. Taig called him an unsavory name, drawing startled glances from his men, but a reluctant grin from Marlin.

"This is what we do, Marlin. It's safer to have any non-military away from harm."

Correct, but Marlin wasn't just anyone. He was an administrative government employee whose position required he interact with several key leaders on Enotia and though not a soldier in the military or an elite Jutak, he was comfortable with the use of weapons from the mandatory classes he'd taken.

When it came to his Chosen, his security clearance more than covered his lack of direct military expertise. "Do what you need to do, Taig, and I'll do what I need to do."

A rough exhale was his only response as the men with Taig pulled their knitted face masks down, once more obscuring their features. "Stubborn *ebo*."

The insult flew over Marlin's head. He'd been called worst. Taig unsnapped the holster on his left thigh and whipped out a wicked sharp knife, passing it to Marlin. The leather grip was firm in his hand. Next Taig reached into one of the many pockets on his pants and passed over a small black circle. Marlin closed his fingers around the spare comm.

Without another word, Taig whirled his pointer finger in a circle and the four men with him eased out of the door, steps quiet despite their large statures.

Marlin waited a beat to give them time then slid out as well. The hallways on this floor were now clear, an unnatural emptiness given the earlier crowd and excitement of the day's event. Marlin timed his approach toward the floor below this one, pausing every few feet until he reached the lobby and central entrance. As he drew close, distant murmurs hinted at the attackers' progress.

At the bottom of the stairs, Marlin ducked behind the thick pillars and rises which made up the grand staircase. The intruders rounded up any visitors caught in the open. An occasional sharp feminine cry or muffled male groan filtered from the other side of his hiding spot. Not knowing if Shaya was among them was like a dagger to the chest, causing Marlin's heart to stutter. He leaned his back against the wall for support. *My Chosen, my Chosen. Stay safe.*

Tension creasing his shoulders, Marlin inhaled deeply then released on a breath and hustled forward. A little farther down the hall and he'd be in full view of anyone coming into the double foyer of the main entry, one on each side of the hall. There were two large rooms in this area often used for charity events or hosting an evening celebration. Both doors were currently closed, leaving no sign as to which was in use.

After digging in his pocket, Marlin pulled out the round disk and looped the thin wire about his lobe, pushing the small comm into his ear.

"Dining hall clear," a cold voice stated.

"Conference room three has guests hiding. Moving to secure location on the next floor."

"Confirmed." Taig's voice he easily recognized.

Marlin was grateful his friend was the Team Leader in charge of the Jutak warriors presenting today. He trusted him to get everyone through whatever this was safely. If anyone could get all of the visitors out of this hostage situation alive, it was Taig. He didn't understand the meaning of defeat.

Now that Marlin knew what areas they were covering, he could proceed with checking these two larger rooms. The elaborate light fixtures above with their multifaceted tubing would leave him completely exposed with little defense once he stepped from behind the staircase.

Running through various scenarios left him with the same option. There really was no other choice. Marlin crept forward, feet silent on the rich red carpet.

Traces of dirt spattered the floor in a dizzying pattern from an overturned planter. Marlin stepped over the shards carefully and moved on. The risk, if caught, meant potential death. His. Even the thought of losing his life didn't deter him. Marlin had only to think of his family and he was resigned to his path.

His grip tightened on the knife Taig had handed him. He was thankful to have a weapon. If a fight erupted, he'd have some form of protection.

Muting the comm to eliminate distraction, Marlin reached the first door, a quick glance around assured he was still alone in the vast lobby. Slowly he extended his hand to twist the metallic yellow knob. Not a creak or squeak. Adrenaline shot pulses racing through his chest. Marlin braced himself for what he might see on the other side and pushed it open all the way.

Empty.

He collapsed against the frame, eyes closed, and let the emotions crash through him until his nerves settled again. Shoving away from the jamb, he made a quick circuit about the twenty by twenty room, confirming there was no one inside. He was almost back to the door when he heard it. A quiet sniffle from the stack of frames along the wall to his left.

Hefting the knife in case of attack, Marlin strode toward the sound and shoved the stack aside to reveal an elderly woman frozen in place, hands over her blonde head as she stared back.

Marlin dropped to a squat and gripped her shoulder. She trembled beneath his touch. "You're alright. Sorry."

"What h-happened?" Her voice broke on the question.

"I'm not sure, but its best you stay here. Rescue will be on their way." He gave a firm squeeze and rose.

Back in the hall, Marlin flipped the lock before shutting the door. No one was getting in without brute force and hopefully it would give her time to hide or escape if possible. He faced the opposite end of the hall. That left checking the second ballroom. It was the only other space on this level large enough to house a group of people.

He didn't think whoever had stormed into the building were on the second floor because all of the commotion had started on this level of the main floor.

"No one here."

At the brusque comment, Marlin ducked behind an alcove and a potted tree decoration just in time. An individual dressed in unrelenting black carrying a heavy duty automated laser walked up the hall in his direction.

"There is no one else on this floor. I sent Wes and Carden to check upstairs, but neither is answering their portable communicators."

Taig and his soldiers probably had something to do with that. At least that was what Marlin hoped as the two opened the door to the room he'd been heading for. A burst of conversation came out which was quickly muffled by the closing of the door behind them.

Marlin waited for the count of five then commed Taig directly.

"Vorik."

"I believe the intruders have gathered on the lower level in the small scale ballroom. Two by the name of Wes and Carden have been noted as missing for failure to check in."

Taig responded in a hushed murmur. "Confirmed, Alonson. What is your position?"

Marlin eased forward, glancing over his shoulder every few steps until he neared the room where he believed the rest of the guests were being held. "Small scale ballroom, of course. I need to know Shaya is safe."

Taig cursed then the comm fell silent. Marlin pressed his ear to the door and held still. Taig's voice muttered, "Don't get killed, Alonson or I swear it *will* be me Shaya walks toward in the next presentation when this is done."

Unexpectedly a grin crossed Marlin's face. Taig Vorik was a good man, a strong Enotian and a Jutak warrior making a name for himself on the elite force. Even Marlin in his non-combative position managed to hear the whispers about the fearless leader.

"Good luck with that, Taig." Marlin muted the comm and focused on hearing what he could through the door.

***

Shaya eyed Jordan as two of his men entered the room and they began arguing in whispered tones. She couldn't hear any of what they said, but Jordan wasn't pleased. The communicator in his hand buzzed and triumph lit his eyes.

"This is Jordan. Am I speaking with the Prime Minister of Enotia?"

The response must have been what he wanted to hear because Jordan grinned and signaled to the two others who also smiled broadly, a congratulatory look passing amongst them. Jordan's voice carried on his demand.

"I want the prisoner, Arid Samba, released to our care. He is not to be transported to Dorlo, the prison colony."

Shaya couldn't believe what she was hearing. Arid was the distant relative of an Enotian woman from off world. He'd come to Enotian in an attempt to hide after his sentencing for unspeakable crimes. Thanks to the bounty alert flashing his holo-image everywhere, he'd been caught and was being held until guards from the judicial system arrived to take him to Dorlo.

A few minutes more talking and Jordan's glee turned, his expression darkening as his lips pressed tight. "What are you saying, Prime Minister?"

A harsh curse and then Jordan stabbed his finger on the comm ending the communication. When he lifted his gaze to scan the crowd, Shaya was sure she wasn't the only one who flinched from the cruelty twisting his mouth.

He raised his weapon and gestured to his three partners then the gathered crowd. "It seems Enotia does not understand what I am willing to do in order to get what I want. Arid will *not* suffer locked away on a vicious prison colony subjected to all manners of maltreatment."

Jordan snarled the last, spittle gathering at the corners of his mouth. He stormed closer and pointed at a trembling female hovering in a corner, shoulders hunched in her pretty bright top as she tried to shrink away.

"You, come forward. For every delay in freeing Arid, I will harm the hostages." He flicked his finger on the comm and placed it to his ear while one of his men dragged the crying woman forward.

Shaya bit her bottom lip, hands knotted at her side. Her body vibrated with the need to act, to do something to stop this madness.

Jordan held up his communicator and activated the vid option. He pointed at the female who'd been forced to her knees in front of him. "Can you see her, Prime Minister Revin?"

The Prime Minister's voice was clear and crisp as he cautiously answered, "Yes."

Jordan nodded. Without another word, the one with his hand clamped around the female's throat, used his other hand to slam the butt of his laser down on her head twice. Blood burst in a startling pattern at her temple as she cried out. Another slam and she fell forward on her hands while the intruder followed her forward and beat her several more times until she lay whimpering on the floor.

Jordan angled the comm in his direction to face the Prime Minister. "Do you understand me now? Every delay will mean your approval to hurt the citizens here. I will not be denied!"

"You have made your point. I will contact the authorities and find where Arid Samba is at this time."

"And arrange for his release!" Jordan snapped. The knuckles of his hand holding the comm turned white as he gripped it. "You have ten minutes to contact me at this comm and confirm that Arid is free and ready to go with us. No tricks or I will shoot to kill."

Those around her gasped and choked back cries. After that pronouncement, Jordan threw the comm on the floor. It was sheer luck it didn't crack as he raked a hand through his hair and began pacing. Two of the guards watched him with neutral expressions while the third who had been tasked with the abuse, pushed the sniveling female back toward them then placed his boot on her back for good measure and kicked.

Several Enotians rushed forward and pulled her into their midst.

Unbelievable. Shaya nibbled at her thumbnail and tried to review best case scenarios in her head. Marlin always said there was an alternative for every action. One just had to think and the answer would be there.

Right now Shaya wasn't sure of anything except the need to survive and to make sure each and everyone of these men paid for the terror they instilled this day.

Chapter 4

The band on Shaya's left wrist buzzed. Checking first to make sure no one noticed, she glanced down at her portable comm. It was Marlin's code. She silenced the vibrating option, wishing with all her heart she could answer her Chosen. With fear radiating from everyone and the air in the room growing stale and stiff, she didn't dare attempt a hushed message to him.

Leaning back against the wall from her seated position on the floor, she confirmed the two minutes left on Jordan's threat. Around her, everyone had also dropped to the floor in wilted slumps against the wall or stretched all out on the floor.

Sweat glistened many brows, her own shirt damp beneath her arms and at the center of her back. The outfit she'd selected for the day was attractive but not meant for a sustained period in a closed environment with failed temperature controls.

"Why is it so hot in here? Where are Wes and Carden? The Prime Minister has one minute left!"

Jordan's comments grew louder as he walked back and forth in front of them with his hands clenched at his sides. He'd reclaimed his comm from the floor and had it tucked in a front pocket of his pants.

Shaya discretely wiped at the sweat on her face. The room had grown progressively hotter. She could only assume it was an action taken by the officials in an attempt to unnerve or discomfit Jordan and the intruders.

One of the three men cornered Jordan and Shaya could hear each word from her position. Others probably could as well.

"Wes and Craven haven't answered comms since we came in. Should I go and look for them?"

Jordan stopped, spun around and scanned the crowd. Shaya jolted when his gaze met hers. "You! Get over here."

Straightening her shoulders and refusing to be intimidated, Shaya made her way toward him. "Yes?"

"Are there Jutaks in the building?"

Shaya froze, not expecting the question. Obviously, there was a Jutak warrior team in the building since one of the exhibitions today had featured them. Was Jordan not aware? Perhaps he assumed that this celebration didn't involve one of Enotia's top military talent.

Blood thundered through her veins. A dose of adrenaline surged as well to make it a high inducing cocktail. Clearing her throat, Shaya took a steadying breath then looked him directly in the eyes and lied. "No."

Jordan stared, his green eyes piercing her with intensity for an uncomfortably long time. More sweat beaded along her arms, leaving her skin sticky.

"No?" Jordan repeated with an arched flame-colored brow.

"No," Shaya stated firmly. She would do nothing to jeopardize the team which could be attempting to rescue them at this very moment.

Jordan continued to glare and Shaya breathed evenly, meeting him stare for stare. If having children had taught her nothing else, she was excellent at unrelenting eye contact.

Without looking away from her face, Jordan held up his hand, signaling the attention of one of his men. "Maris, check on Wes and Craven. And find out why the ventilation system is suddenly not working."

"Right away."

Maris, the dark-haired one, darted out of the room and the door clicked shut behind him.

Jordan's upper lip curled and Shaya prepared herself for a physical attack or verbal assault. Doubt flickered in his gaze the longer he focused his attention on her. Relief arrived in the form of the ding from the comm in his hand. Jordan glanced away, breaking the contact and Shaya exhaled in relief though she kept her expression neutral.

"Prime Minister Revin, have you decided to agree to my request?" he asked in a dark tone.

Breath suspended, Shaya waited. Laughter exploded from Jordan as he walked away from her. He slid his free hand into his pocket and tapped his foot in an uneven beat. "Good. I was sure you would see things my way. Have Arid waiting at the station. No guards or others with him. He will be leaving on a shuttle arriving shortly."

Jordan ended the call and the remaining two males with him whistled loudly. They joined Jordan to clap him on the back, sneering about the authorities and Enotia in general. The cheerful circle lasted a bit until Jordan's head snapped up. His gaze narrowed on Shaya. Then he spun toward the door.

"Why isn't Maris back?"

His compatriots frowned, hands holding their lasers tightly as they all waited for the door to open. Jordan spoke into his comm. "Maris, check in."

Silence.

Rumbles grew and fanned out behind her, but Shaya didn't dare turn to take in everyone's reactions. Her heart sped up and it took every bit of nerve she possessed to maintain her composure. Deep inside she hoped her Chosen was doing whatever possible to see to their children.

"Maris!" Jordan barked into the comm a second time. Then a third. "Maris, check in!"

"Should I look for him, Jordan?" The blond male on the left asked, his face pale as he awkwardly shuffled on his feet.

"Yes. You and Keet." Jordan tagged the male on his right. As he waited for them to reach the door, Jordan added, "Shoot anyone who dares to get in your way."

He flicked a glance at Shaya. "I will do the same if you are involved in this."

Shaya swallowed. "I have been in here the entire time. I am not at fault for anything that may or may not have happened."

Before she could move, Jordan strode toward her and struck. The smack resounded as the flat of his hand connected with her cheek. Several gasps filled the air. Shaya staggered back on one foot then surged forward. Her fist swung of its own accord and she punched him right in the face. Instinctively, she'd planted her weight behind the blow as Marlin had taught her. Jordan dropped to a knee and cursed as he spit blood onto the polished flooring.

Pain lit Shaya's knuckles after the fact. She cradled her sore fist close to her chest and waited.

Head bowed, Jordan chuckled roughly. He smoothed back his hair with a glide of his palm and stood. Shaya retreated back a few steps in self-preservation.

"What is your name?"

While his tone was reasonable, the look in his eyes was not. The green orbs burned with fury. A violent flush stained his cheeks a deep red. Her gaze was drawn to the single drop of blood formed on his top lip where she must have cut him.

"Your name!" he roared when she failed to answer.

"Shaya." It was all she dared say on the off chance he was aware of Marlin and his affiliation with the government.

Jordan closed the distance between them and cupped the back of Shaya's head with one hand and the laser hit her hip as he planted his other hand at her waist. Heart pounding out a rapid beat, Shaya stilled in the odd embrace. Jordan lowered his head and whispered directly in her ear. "If my men do not return, you will be the first I kill."

She flinched, then jerked from his hold and snarled, "Good luck."

It was a bold thing to say. Shaya knew it, but she also didn't plan to let him terrorize her.

***

When the sound of steps neared the door, Marlin backed up and kept his knife down by his thigh. The door opened and a lone figure exited. Marlin was on him in an instant, an arm going about his opponent's throat as he forced him to the floor then straddled him.

The male below him thrashed and opened his mouth. Marlin slapped a palm over his mouth and pressed the blade to the sensitive curve of his neck and whispered, "Do not."

The criminal stilled. Marlin leaned lower. "How many are with you?"

He eased his hand away slightly for a response. The male gritted out, "It will do you no good. Any attempt will result in loss of life. Are you willing to risk that?"

Marlin growled and dragged him to his feet, hand clamped around the other male's mouth. Behind him the whisper of fabric on air had Marlin tensing. When he turned, Taig strode toward him along with another of his team. Both had their faces covered but years of friendship would always enable Marlin to recognize Taig's body language.

Without exchanging a word, Taig removed a pair of flexi-cuffs from the loop at his waist and slid them on the intruder and jammed a gag in his mouth before shoving him toward his teammate roughly.

"What have you got, Alonson?"

Marlon rolled his eyes though his lips twitched. "I was just about to question him further."

As if realizing their whispers might carry, Taig tipped his head back in the direction he'd come. They hustled down the hall and back to the closet of earlier. Taig tapped his ear comm. "Ballroom, first floor. Need eyes, now!"

All of them gazed at the restrained, and surprisingly docile male.

"How many are with you?" Taig asked.

He shrugged, a slight smirk curling his lips.

Marlin had to resist the urge to put his hands on him. With every budding second, he was more and more certain Shaya was in there with a volatile criminal. After leaving the cleansing room, her first stop would have been the auditorium, seeking him and their children when the attack started.

Marlin kicked at the lower shelving, causing the items to rattle. Taig glared. Marlin didn't care. He got in the face of the cuffed prisoner and snatched the gag from his mouth. "Do not think my peaceful ways make me opposed to hurting you. Who are you with? What are you doing with the Enotians inside?"

Fear skittered across the male's features. "Jordan wants Arid Samba freed."

Marlin froze. Not because the name Jordan meant anything to him. It was the Arid Samba connection that had the blood draining from his face. Arid had been picked up earlier this morning by authorities for transport to a prison planet. Marlin had witnessed and signed the communication when it crossed his desk late the evening before.

"Knock him out," Taig directed at his man.

The other Jutak warrior crouched behind the prisoner and pressed a small cylinder to his throat. He slumped over on a weak cry.

"I have the Prime Minister on a private comm channel and the Jutak Commander. Arid Samba is not here. There is no way they can meet this Jordan's demands, Marlin," Taig rattled off.

"What does that mean exactly?"

Taig shook his head, spoke a few words to those on the other end of the comm then met Marlin's gaze. "There were six attackers. Including this one we have three in custody. We were also able to shut down the temp controls. But none of that will help since my team has been instructed to stand down until another Jutak team can arrive to assist."

And have Shaya wait longer? Risk his Chosen on a whim?

"That is not an option, Taig," Marlin said simply.

Taig ripped the black knit mask from his face. A muscle ticked in his prominent jaw. "You don't think I'm worried about Shaya too, Marlin?!"

It took effort, but Marlin remained calm. "Then you know we can't wait. Think of what you know of Shaya, Taig. How long do you think she will last before she attempts to help by stopping this Jordan herself?"

The Jutak warrior with them snickered. "I am envious. She sounds like a worthy female."

"She is," Taig and Marlin both answered.

Ignoring the evidence that his friend had still not gotten over his infatuation with Shaya, Marlin snarled and slammed his fist into the wall behind him. "I am not waiting, Taig."

They all tensed at the slight cracking sound. One beat, two. No shouts or alarms rang out.

"There may be something." Taig paused and stared at the floor as he focused. "Opening the line for the spare comm so Alonson can hear."

A click and Marlin's earbud opened mid-conversation. It was the rest of Taig's Jutak warrior teammates located somewhere in the building. "We have apprehended two more of the intruders. According to their statements only the leader and another resides in the ballroom. Two weapons between them and roughly fifty hostages from today's event."

Pleasure creased Taig's face. "Perfect. Make sure they are secure and meet back in the position from earlier."

The closet was about to get a lot more crowded.

Taig faced Marlin. "While we wait, do you have any way to contact Shaya?"

Marlin didn't have to strain his memory. He distinctly remembered her wearing it on her left wrist after they'd sex shared in the shower. "Her comm. She usually keeps it on vibrate."

Taig's smile widened. "This is turning out better than we could have hoped. Comm Shaya."

Marlin pulled out his handheld communication device and signaled Shaya's comm. He raised the volume so they could all listen in. It clicked several times, but no answer. Disappointment swelled. "She didn't answer earlier either."

Taig shook his head. "No worries. It would have been too easy to think she could answer safely. Does she have messaging capability?"

Marlin was already tapping out a brief message to Shaya when a single line scrolled over the tiny screen. *'I love you and Torkel and Lissi very much.'*

Cramps seized his stomach and pure adrenaline rushed through Marlin's veins. HE showed his friend. "We need to act now."

Taig stared. Without asking Marlin any question, he pointed at the Jutak warrior with them. "Stay here and watch him."

Then he flicked his fingers at Marlin and the door. "Go."

Marlin snatched the door open and came face to face with the remaining three Jutak warriors from Taig's team. Between them were two bound males, faces flushed and hair in disarray.

Taig took charge. "Asaan, Rordan with me. Adin stay and help cover the prisoners."

Marlin's heart tripped, but he followed Taig and the other two. For large males, their steps were light and if not for Marlin would have gone unheard. Fortunately, the main hall was empty when they arrived. With his back to the wall, Taig scanned the hall once more before pointing toward his teammates then the ceiling. "Go up. Try the vent system and see if you can get us a view into that room."

Brisk nods and then they disappeared around the corner.

"What are you thinking?" Marlin asked when it was just the two of them.

"I need to know the positioning of this Jordan. Asaan and Rordan are sniper level. If possible, they can end this standoff with a single shot and everyone walks away alive today."

Marlin fervently hoped that was true. The comm in his ear activated.

"Slight problem, Team Leader."

"Go," Taig said.

"The target has a female too close to risk the shot."

It had to be his Chosen. A sinking sensation swirled in his belly as he whispered, "Shaya."

Chapter 5

The glint from one of the grates in the ceiling caught Shaya's attention. Without moving her head, she risked a quick glance up. Her position was too precarious for anything more.

"Answer me! Anyone!"

Jordan kept a tight grasp about Shaya's neck, his eyes on his comm as he waited for a response from his people. The silence was thick enough to coat Shaya's tongue in terror. Fury drew the skin over his cheeks taut, making the bones of his face stand out in stark relief.

He lowered his comm to his side and tightened the fingers of his free hand around Shaya's throat. Her pulse leaped and tapped a desperate beat against her skin. Jordan turned slowly to face her. Shaya gathered her courage, prepared to do whatever necessary to stop Jordan.

"Looks like you have an appointment with destiny today," he growled.

A shiver rolled down her spine. Working her throat, she took a moment to speak due to the pressure from his hand. "You have one too."

His brow crinkled as he tried to puzzle her remark. Shaya jerked hard at his hold and brought her hands up to slam her palms on the sides of his head. In the same motion, she brought up her knee and slammed it as hard as she could at the region of his crotch.

He roared and released her as he bent over. Shaya rolled as soon as she was free and pushed herself backward as far as she could. The grate above fell to the floor with a clatter and the *zip zip* of a laser sounded. Jordan dropped beside the grate on a scream.

"Jutak warriors! Jutak warriors!"

Two black-clad figures rappelled down from a black cord and hit the floor at a run. They had Jordan covered immediately. One kicked out to turn him on his back and the other aimed his weapon at Jordan's head.

Shaya rose shakily to her feet. All around chaos erupted as some slowly realized they'd been saved. The door banged open and a male stormed toward her. Blond hair and blue eyes filled with concern. Her Chosen swooped her up in his arms as soon as he reached her side.

"Shaya."

Her name was muffled as he buried his face against her throat and held her in a vise-like grip about her waist. His big body shuddered against her.

Shaya calmed her own heart rate and smoothed a hand up his back. "Please tell me the children are safe."

Marlin lifted his head and tears glinted in his gaze. "Yes. They're locked in my office. I sent them away as soon as I realized something was wrong."

The last of her tension drained away and Shaya slumped in his arms, her own grip tight about his shoulders. "I was worried."

With a weak laugh, Marlin pulled back slightly. "*You* were worried?"

Shaya grinned. "It is different being on one end and not knowing if my family was safe."

"Same." Marlin smoothed a shaking hand over her hair which was probably an awful mess now.

"We need to get them. I can not imagine how afraid they are."

He nodded.

"Shaya Redenler."

Shaya turned at the voice. It was somehow familiar, but she couldn't place the tall dark clad figure. Weapons were strapped to both of his thighs, his tread silent as he crossed the room toward them. The black mask hid his features, all except stern blue eyes.

A Jutak warrior.

"Shaya Alonson." Had been for some years, so it was odd hearing someone call her by her old name.

He inclined his head in acknowledgment of the correction. "I am glad to see you safe."

She tried to pierce the mystery of his face behind the fabric.

Marlin leaned close. "My friend, Taig Vorik. You remember him?"

Vaguely. Instead of revealing her doubt, she offered her appreciation for his actions today. "Thank you. And the other Jutaks."

"It is our duty." He continued to watch her with an unblinking blue gaze until Jordan groaned from behind them.

Taig became all business and slapped Marlin on the back. "You were always lucky, Alonson."

He began ordering the Jutak warriors gathered and they jumped to obey. Injuries were seen to, the wounded being escorted out where medical help awaited, Shaya presumed. Others were assisted to their feet and escorted through the open door. Once finished, the four soldiers returned to lead a docile Jordan from the ballroom.

Taig, Marlin's friend, approached the murmuring guests and at that point Shaya lost interest. She had only one goal in mind. "I want to get my babies and go home."

"Absolutely." Marlin wrapped his arm about her lower back and walked her from the room.

***

Shaya wasn't sure who was more excited when their family was reunited. Torkel and Lissi's faces beamed the entire ride home to their farm. Because of the eventful day, she suggested they eat the pastry treat she'd been saving for a special occasion and pushed dinner back for later.

The excitement kept the conversation flowing until Shaya noticed their eyes drooping at the table. "I think it is bedtime."

For once they didn't moan or groan. Marlin carried Lissi who was already half-sleep and Shaya held Torkel's hand as she led him to his bedroom. It was as she was tucking the covers about his shoulders that he reached out and clasped her hand.

Shaya smiled. "What is it, Torkel?"

"I was really scared." He said it as if he was ashamed of the admission.

Shaya brushed back the long strands of his dark brown hair. "Do you want to know something?"

He nodded, his eyes bright with curiosity.

"So was I. I was scared for you and your sister and I was scared for your papan."

The floor behind her creaked and her Chosen sat down on the edge of Torkel's bed next to them. "Is everything alright?"

"Torkel was sharing his fear about today." Shaya stroked a hand down her son's arm to soothe whatever had put the worried look in his wide eyes.

"Is there anything we can do to help you, Torkel? Do you want to talk about things?" Marlin asked.

The gentle tone he used as he voiced the questions left Shaya's heart melting. She leaned back against her Chosen and he scooted closer, so they presented a united front for their son.

Torkel licked his lips, his gaze darting around nervously before he blurted. "I was really scared because I thought it was the Marenians. I thought they had come back to take me away."

Shaya's breath froze in her chest. She was at once crushed and angered. Crushed because she couldn't tell if this was something Torkel worried over but also angry that Jordan and his band of criminals had brought such a fear to the forefront of their son's mind.

Marlin ever calm leaned around her and placed his large hand on the side of Torkel's face. "Were you scared in a good way like you wanted to go or in a bad way like you did not want to go?"

Waiting for the answer had Shaya almost in tears. Torkel was their first. Maybe not the child of her blood but the child of her heart in every way that counted and she'd kill anyone who thought to take him away from her.

"In a bad way," Torkel whispered, slouching low in his bed covers.

"I think it is time your maman and I told you all the details of how you came to us and made us a family."

Shaya glanced up meeting Marlin's gaze. "Everything?"

His lips quirked. "Everything."

She huffed. "I stand by all of my actions during that time."

Torkel sat up in the bed and while his fear hadn't completely faded he looked intrigued. And so they told him how they'd found him abandoned on the farm which he already knew. They told him about the adoption center, how the workers lost the few belongings left with him. And in the end with great glee, Marlin told him about how Shaya had almost been arrested stealing him.

Torkel looked at her with shock. "Maman!"

Shaya wrapped her arms around him and squeezed tight. He'd had a growth spurt recently and was now considered large for his age. No longer the scrawny boy Lissi had been able to push about. At least, he'd yet to show signs that he didn't want his maman's physical affection. "You are mine, Torkel Alonson. Never doubt it."

When they turned the light out and left his room, there was a small smile on Torkel's face that eased any concern Shaya may have had. In their bedroom as she undressed she asked Marlin, "Do you think we have to worry about his family coming back for him?"

"We are his family." Marlin tugged his shirt over his head.

His muscled chest distracted from her line of questioning. He walked to the closet and removed the rest of his clothing. When he re-entered the bedroom, he was completely naked and had a gleam in his eyes. Shaya settled back against the pillows in their bed, eager to wait and see his intentions.

Marlin leaned one knee on the bed and slid beneath the covers. He curled on his side facing her and cupped her cheek. "You cannot imagine the terror I felt when I knew you had to be one of the hostages."

Shaya placed her hand over his and squeezed. "All of it was a frightening experience. Let us try and put it in the past. Jordan will face justice for his actions along with the others and Arid Samba was not freed."

"Which is good news." Marlin nipped her bottom lip.

Sensations stirred and her lower region clenched with desire. Shaya eased her knee between his thighs and nudged. "Very."

His gasp sent a thrill through her. Running a hand over his hip, Shaya moved closer and kissed him. Marlin groaned and slid his arm under her to pull her against him. Her nipples brushed his solid chest and became tiny points. A moan slipped past her lips.

Desperate to erase the events of today from her memory with her Chosen's touch, Shaya pressed her mouth to his.

On a groan, Marlin gripped her hair and tugged as he broke the kiss. "Do you truly not remember my friend Taig?"

Shaya paused. She vaguely recalled the name, but now as she matched it with the eyes of the Jutak warrior from earlier, she said, "I think I do. You were close."

Chapter 6

Marlin laughed uproariously and snatched his Chosen up as he rolled to his back and propped her on top of him. When he settled and his mirth died down, he stared into her confused gaze. "We are still close. He is a very dear friend but because of his work with the Jutaks, we don't get to see each other often any more."

Not much at all since they'd entered presentation together with the hopes of catching the same woman's eyes.

Shaya nodded. Marlin held in a snicker at the disinterest on her face. Taig might think he still had a chance if Marlin wasn't a factor but it was evident his love had no interest in him. Leaning up, he kissed her pert nose, chin and then teased her lips with his tongue. Shaya's mouth parted and Marlin spent the next few moments memorizing her taste and languishing in the pleasure having her in his arms brought.

Slowly he rocked his hips up and Shaya undulated over him, moisture trickling between their thighs. Marlin smoothed his hands down her back and then up. He did it again until he cupped her round cheeks in his palms. He squeezed and grinned as she arched and broke the kiss.

"About Torkel. Do we need to be worried about losing him?" Tension lined her body, removing the sensual spell entwining them.

Marlin gave it serious thought because he saw the worry on her face. "I think he was left here for a reason. Maybe they knew what a good maman you would be." She melted against him. "Maybe they wanted him somewhere safe. Whatever brought him into our lives, I am grateful and will love him and fight for him."

Shaya grinned. Her hands reached down as she stroked his twitching cock. "You're right. I won't think of it any more."

She lifted her hips and slowly lowered herself onto his erection. Marlin threw his head back on the pillows as her warm, wet center gloved him from tip to base. Then she tortured him with fast gyrations mixed with slow hip swivels. He held her hips tight for the ride and as his climax exploded, he groaned deep in his throat.

Shaya collapsed atop him having timed her orgasm to his own. Something she often did with amazing accuracy. Kissing his chest as she dozed, Shaya murmured, "Taig Vorik never stood a chance."

And Marlin fell asleep with a smile on his face, arms tight around the woman he loved.

Author's Note

This was a delight to write. I never thought much about Shaya and Marlin other than they are awesome amazing parents and I love them so hard. LOL. Then I sat down and suddenly I "saw" this moment in time for them with Torkel and Lissi as kids.

At first, I thought this would be a coming of age from Torkel's point of view and how he became a Jutak but Shaya and Marlin's story unfolded and I couldn't pull away. Hopefully, everyone enjoyed this glimpse into their past since Shaya has quite the fan group of her own.

And yes, at some point in one of the upcoming books we will learn more about how Torkel, a baby of Marenian descent, ended up on Enotia and specifically on Marlin and Shaya's farm.

Michelle H.

Better Every Time

A World Beyond Novella

By Michelle Howard

Published by MH Publications

Chapter 1

"The meeting is hereby closed unless anyone has another point of interest." High Councilor Jakil paused to scan the room of Senate Leaders.

No one spoke or raised a hand for an extension of the meeting they had been required to attend. Baruk breathed a sigh of relief, excited at the thought of going home on time for the first time in weeks.

It was rare any of their presence was deemed necessary at the Senate Hall more than once a week, but today's agenda had included finalizing details on several grant proposals for the government which had been argued over to the point tempers had exploded. They'd fought over every section and article until settling on a firm resolution they could all agree to.

"Meeting officially completed. Please note the time." The High Councilor stepped away from the head of the table, his black ankle length senate robes swaying with his movement.

Several Senate Leaders rose to their feet and broke off into smaller groups. Baruk was thinking of the easiest way to ease out the door without being caught in any of those conversations. He wanted to get back to his wife and their children.

"Why don't you just walk out?"

The deep rumbling voice behind him was heavy with amusement. Baruk composed his features before turning to face a man he'd grown to not only tolerate but like and respect. His spouse partner and fellow Senate Leader, Zadal.

"If I rush out, it is guaranteed to cause one of them to call out my name with an urgent discussion that absolutely must occur now."

Zadal's mouth twisted in a familiar cynical smile. He rocked back on his heels, shoving his hands into the pockets of his senate robes and declared. "Best of luck. I'm leaving. I miss Lindsey and the girls."

With that, he turned away and strode straight for the door. Only two Senate Leaders attempted to stop him by boldly calling out his name as he crossed the room thus drawing attention from the others who chimed in. Zadal ignored them all and promptly opened the door and took his leave. But not without tossing a smirk over his shoulder at Baruk.

Stunned, he simply stared. Only Zadal could have made it look that easy. Gathering his wits, Baruk snatched his data pad from the table with every intention of following suit.

"Senate Leader Baruk."

Someone called his name when he was only a few steps from the door. Baruk blew out a breath and hung his head. He should have known it wouldn't work. While many of his colleagues had grown to accept his spouse partner, Zadal, many of them still avoided doing anything to draw his ire.

Zadal had a temper and as the *briot* son of a sex-service worker, he'd fought long and hard for acceptance among his peers and didn't forgive them their initial slight of him. Though Baruk had never had a true problem with Zadal. At the time, the brutish blond with a grudge had already showed signs of being an exemplary Senate Leader even when they bumped heads and voted against one another on zoning or policy. As a spouse partner, Zadal more than fit in the marital Triad Baruk was a part of.

Giving his attention to the man who now stood at his side, Baruk asked, "What can I do for you, Maro?"

As Maro launched into a long winded speech, Baruk gave up on any plans to get out of here early and spend time with his enchanting wife. Which meant Zadal would have all the fun this evening.

***

One, two, three. Three babies huddled together in sleep. His daughters. Part of his family now. Zadal stared at the little bundles curled side by side in their bed. He dismissed the house assistant whose responsibility strictly consisted of helping his wife, Lindsey, so she wouldn't feel overrun.

"Are you sure Senate Leader Gatar?" Graeme asked.

"Positive." Zadal waved his hand, sending the man on his way to another part of the vast Laars estate which had been in Baruk's family for years.

Graeme left with a wide grin, amused no doubt by Zadal's constant visits to the nursery to see the babies. The door closed behind him with a gentle thud and only one of the babies flinched at the noise before settling.

It was times like these, Zadal cherished the most. The quiet and ability to focus in complete fascination on the fact that he'd had a part in creating something good and beautiful. His life had not always been that way. He was the bastard son of a woman who sold her body for *likos*. Zadal could have accepted that—no one understood survival of the fittest more than him but Aiella Gatar had made his life unnecessarily difficult.

First with her refusal to disclose the name of his father, increasing his stigma among their people who labeled him the derogatory term *briot* and then with her recreational drug use that sent her into uncontrollable rages.

The struggles, the beatings, it all had an impact on his outlook on life. Not once as a child had he been tempted to follow in his mother's steps by succumbing to a life of misery and illegal activity. Fate had chosen to give Zadal a different path, a better path and he'd taken the chance to do more for himself by gripping every opportunity that came his way with determination and sheer stubbornness to succeed.

Now he had a spouse partner whom he respected and admired though he still enjoyed taunting Baruk. Like earlier today when he'd left him at work. Zadal toyed with a blonde curl on Briar's head and smiled in remembrance at Baruk's shock. At some point, Baruk would try and retaliate and Zadal reluctantly admitted to looking forward to it.

The prickly games they played were harmless and had actually drawn them closer. Without a doubt Zadal considered Baruk a friend and knew he'd stand by him regardless of anything that came their way.

That didn't mean he didn't still envy his spouse partner occasionally. Baruk came from a background of wealth and privilege. He'd had parents who loved him and grown in a secure environment never fearing for his life as Zadal had. In spite of that or maybe despite it, Baruk was as solid as they came.

"Hey, I didn't know you were home."

At the perk greeting, Zadal glanced up to see his wife bounce in. Hair pulled back in a tail, face free of cosmetic enhancements and wearing a sleeping gown of rich blue belted at the waist, her appearance stirred his arousal and the beginning of an erection stiffened his cock.

"Hello, Lindsey."

She yawned continuing toward him, creases on her cheeks hinting she'd just come from her bed. He knew since he'd checked before coming to see the babies and been reluctant to wake her.

"Are you okay? How was work?" When she reached him, Lindsey leaned her weight against his side and wrapped one arm about his waist as he dutifully lowered his head for her to kiss his forehead.

Relaxing into her touch, Zadal closed his eyes and inhaled her familiar scent. Probably a gift from Baruk. He was good about buying her things like that while Zadal was more likely to stumble around and rely on his first assistant Beline to suggest something appropriate. "I'm fine. Work went well."

In the beginning, he hadn't known how to handle Lindsey's exuberance and open affection. Zadal wrapped an arm about her hips and tugged her to his front. Now he wouldn't know what to do without it.

She rested her head on his chest and stroked a hand through his hair. "Where is Baruk? Didn't he come home with you?"

Her question brought a return to his earlier smile as he said with glee, "He stopped to speak with a few others."

Lindsey frowned and leaned back to see his face clearly. "You both have been working so hard these last weeks. I was sure he wanted to come home early today but maybe I was mistaken."

Shaking her head in dismay, she angled her body so they could both stare into the baby bed at their children. "They look so peaceful. You'd never know this morning Azalea wouldn't settle down and screamed until she turned red in the face and choked. Briar joined her resulting in hiccups, poor sweetie. Lucky for Graeme and me, Camille slept through it all."

Azalea, Briar and Camille. Flower names.

Because Baruk loved horticulture and every aspect of gardening. Though Camille's namesake was a thieving criminal without a drop of honor in him, he was also one of Lindsey's closest friends whom she refused to end contact with.

As to the other girls, Zadal was a little put out to know she'd named the children in a way to honor his spouse partner. He knew Lindsey loved him. Had no doubt in his mind actually. But there were still moments like now where Zadal questioned if she preferred her other husband to him.

Lindsey ran a hand up his back "Z, what's going on? You seem miles away."

Z. He hid a wince at the dreaded short name and stepped away from the babies' bed after one last stroke against a tiny curled fist. "Nothing."

Lindsey followed him into the hall and caught the back of his black senate robes, preventing his escape to his bedroom. "Don't lie to me. Anything but that. If now is not a good time, say it, but I'm too sensitive for lies between any of us."

Because she'd been kidnapped and led to believe he and Baruk didn't want her. Zadal sighed and gripped the back of his neck. She didn't deserve his frustration or his issues with his self worth. "It's just that I didn't expect there was more to your desire to use Earth names for the babies. Knowing you chose them with Baruk in mind brought up bad memories."

Her mouth curved in a soft smile. She slid in front of him and wrapped her arms about him. Zadal returned the embrace automatically. There was nothing better than hugging his wife. Lindsey was ever sensitive to the nuances of his mood and had been from the early days of their marriage when he questioned his place in their Triad. Like now.

Another rough exhale and Zadal eased back to caress her cheek. "I'm being foolish."

Her brows creased. "Something hurt you though. Something I did."

He denied it with shake of his head. "Not at all."

But she continued to frown and nibbled her bottom lip. Zadal tried to pull from her hold. "I need to shower and change."

Usually he snuck away from his home office to snatch a few moments with their children during the day. He couldn't resist staring at them. Since today was one of the rare times he had to go to the Senate Hall in person, he'd missed his bonding time with them and felt grimy from being out all day.

Lindsey's expression fell as she let him go. "You're not jealous, are you?"

Zadal plastered a fake smile on his face to placate her as he began walking backward down the hall toward his bedroom. "I love our children, Lindsey."

Unconditionally.

Lindsey wagged a finger at him, almost skipping to keep up with his evasive moves. "You silly man."

She ran toward him and jumped, leaving Zadal no choice but to catch her. The sudden weight threw him off balance and he stumbled near the top of the elaborate spiral stairs. Heart in his throat, Zadal spun them to the side and braced her against the wall. "*Verat*, Lindsey! You have to warn me when you do that."

She ignored his muttered complaint to press kisses all over his face. Holding his chin up out of reach, he caught her wrists and brought them down. Not in the least perturbed, Lindsey leaned her weight into him, grinning all the while. "I love *you*. The flower names are to give Baruk an added sense of connection because it's obvious to anyone with eyes the girls are yours."

Zadal braced his forearms against the wall by her head and stared in confusion. "Baruk and I are both their fathers. We told you Garulaxan don't care about paternal genetics."

It wasn't important since all Triad marriages were composed of two husbands and a wife.

Lindsey twisted about until he lowered her feet to the floor and released her. Running her fingers down his face, she cupped his jaw. "It's different in our situation. You and Baruk never would have shared a Triad if it wasn't for me. Of course there will be times when one of you will feel disadvantaged."

Zadal wanted to deny her claim, but knew deep inside it was true. Lindsey kissed him softly, a slight press of her lips to his. "You probably never noticed but Baruk was sad for a few days after the birth of the girls."

He hadn't noticed. Baruk and he had started this relationship as adversaries. Only their love for Lindsey had helped bridge the gap. "Baruk seems fine."

Lindsey snorted. "After we agreed on the names he was happier."

"And?" Zadal had no idea where she was going with this.

Lindsey yanked his hair, causing him to wince. "He could tell you are the girls' natural father. Maybe it doesn't matter to men on your world or maybe just maybe he held hope they'd be his."

"They are!"

Lindsey stared and arched a brow. Zadal's nerves quivered. He didn't put any thought to the girls' paternity because he and Baruk signed the standard marriage agreement foregoing the right to ever know which children possessed their genetics. But *did* Baruk care?

On the surface he seemed to be fine but what if Lindsey was right? Baruk came from a happy loving family. Perhaps a part of him held to an outdated belief in fathering his own.

"Now you get it." Lindsey smoothed her hands down his chest. "The names of our children was something I wanted Baruk to feel was his. Who knows the next one might be his genetically and I'll get to name a little Z."

Blood drained from Zadal's face as he remembered how she'd labored. The fear, the pain. Not only hers but his. Worried something would go wrong had made Zadal sick to the stomach. It was not a process he was in a rush to experience again. He placed his hands over hers on his chest and squeezed. "Tell me you're not pregnant again, Lindsey."

Zadal didn't care how desperate he sounded. The girls were only a few months old. Granted he and Baruk spent every night possible showing Lindsey how much they loved and worshipped her body once she recovered, but he was still adjusting to *having* a family. A spouse partner, wife and children were a huge change for him.

Breaking his hold, Lindsey laughed in his face and stepped back. "No. But obviously we'll have more children later."

More children. The thought slammed into the forefront of his mind. Zadal's heart boomed in his chest as if trying to break free. This was real. This was his life, not a dream. Lighthearted in a way he couldn't express, Zadal swooped Lindsey up into his arms.

Enjoying when she squealed and clutched at him, his steps toward his room were rushed. Zadal burst through the door, not bothering to close it behind him as he placed Lindsey on his bed and dropped on top of her, mindful of his weight.

Her gaze lowered and she teased him by pulling at the black senate robes he still wore. Undoing the clasp to help, he shoved it down his shoulders only for it to catch at his elbows.

"What ever are you doing, Z?"

Hiding his grin, Zadal buried his face in the hollow of her neck and shoulder and bit down. Not enough to hurt, never that, but enough to give an erotic sting of pain. Lindsey shivered beneath him.

***

Zadal nipped and licked as he kissed up and down Lindsey's throat. Each touch of his lips set her skin on fire, leaving goose bumps behind. Sex on Earth had been fun and freeing but sex with her husbands was much more.

"You don't need this," Zadal murmured as he leaned up on his haunches and slid her sleep gown up and over her head.

He nipples beaded into tight buds immediately. His brown gaze heated as he took in her scantily clad body. Lindsey hadn't bothered with a bra and her breasts had retained the fullness of pregnancy boobs with all the sensitivity included. He smoothed a rough palm down her torso and Lindsey couldn't resist arching to the caress.

"I could come so quick." It was the truth. She'd been partially aroused all day and cursed the fact both of her husbands had to leave for work this morning, leaving her frustrated and horny.

"Really," Zadal drawled with a hike of one eyebrow.

Lindsey debated reaffirming her statement but then shrugged. She had no reason to hide how she felt. "I'm extremely wet."

Twin flags of red popped on Zadal's cheeks and his groan was reward enough. She held in a chuckle as he leaped from the bed and tore at his senate robes. Instead of the care he usually gave his clothes, he tossed the black bundle to the floor behind him and yanked the custom white button down over his head.

"Mmm." Lindsey moaned uncontrollably.

Thick and broad, Zadal was built like a muscled tank and Lindsey loved every inch of it. She admired the rest of him as he kicked off his shoes and pants. The black underwear was whisked down his thighs, giving Lindsey an unencumbered view of his twitching cock as he grasped the length and stroked down. The glistening head emerged from the folds of foreskin and her mouth dried in anticipation.

"How wet did you say you were?"

Lindsey trembled. Oh yes, this was the side of her husband she most enjoyed. Dark. Demanding. Zadal approached the bed and stood at the side, rubbing slow and steady up and down his shaft. It pulsed so hard even Lindsey could catch the minute movement.

"Really, really...really wet." She spread her legs in a wanton display she knew neither of her husbands could resist.

Breath hitching, Zadal bit his bottom lip and stroked faster. He stopped at the edge of the bed, his gaze greedy as it roved over her body. "Make me wet too."

Eagerly, Lindsey rolled to her side and balanced on one elbow while she cupped Zadal's firm hold on his shaft. He bumped the head against her mouth and her lips parted as she sucked him deep. The scent of him rose and Lindsey bit back a whimper to focus on the taste of the thick shaft pumping in her mouth.

"Fuck! Yes. Take me deep." Head thrown back, he rocked. Each muscle in his thigh flexed and released with his thrusts.

Adding her tongue, Lindsey alternated flicks with sucks. Zadal yelled and shoved his fingers through her hair, pulling hard. Moisture trickled down her thighs and Lindsey found herself rocking in counterpoint on the bed. As the pleasure overwhelmed, Lindsey closed her eyes. She needed to be filled, wanted his cock inside.

Angling her neck, allowed her to take more of him in her throat. Lindsey toyed with his sac below and fingered the sensitive bumps. She'd learned a lot as the wife in the middle of a Triad. Otherwise her husbands would have long since worn her out.

"Not so fast," Zadal growled as he slowed down. "Open your eyes."

She did. Greed glittered in his gaze. Lindsey swallowed the drops of precum drizzling in her mouth. Zadal pulled out to her disbelief. He chuckled and climbed into the bed, easing her onto her back as he crouched above. "I'm going to be deep inside you when I release."

He pinned her hands to the bed with a solid hold on her wrists and Lindsey thought she'd explode right then. Planting himself between her legs, Zadal adjusted his weight and pushed forward. He was hard enough to penetrate without guidance and her slick channel welcomed him, clenching and quivering until his groin smashed into hers.

Zadal stared down at her. "I'm torn."

"You are?" Lindsey wrapped her thighs around his hips and swiveled the tiniest bit. "Do you need me to tell you what comes next?"

His bark of laughter jiggled both of their bodies and Lindsey bit off a moan. "Tease. I want to suck your nipples and kiss you."

"Do both," Lindsey breathed, her nerves fluttering.

"I do believe I will." He lowered his head and lipped at her right nipple, laving the pink nub then sucking it.

Lindsey was moaning and fighting to get free to touch and stroke at will when he switched to her left breast and gave it the same treatment. Careful licks followed by wet lavish strokes from his tongue and then drawing on her nipple with a powerful sucking motion had Lindsey's orgasm roaring through her.

She screamed and locked her ankles about him as her body pumped upward with aggressive thrusts. Zadal met each one with the fiery snap of his own hips until the bed bounced and the frame slammed into the wall behind them. Again and again until the small bite of pain from the pressure enhanced the flow of pleasure.

Her inner walls clamped down on his length, tightening his passage and Zadal's face dropped down next to hers on a gasp. "*Verat*! Tight, Fucking tight and so good."

Rough pants hit her cheek with his every breath. His body strained, shoulders rocking as he continued to work his way back and forth.

"Fuck me, Z. Fuck me," she encouraged, sweat gathering on their bodies and adding the smack of flesh on flesh to their vocal symphony.

Suddenly he froze, a choked cry rising between them. Then Zadal lost all control, pumping fast and furious before groaning and collapsing on the pillow beside her. Lindsey slumped in relief and satisfaction, her legs sprawling to the bed weakly. Zadal released her wrists to gather her in his arms as he moaned into the side of her neck.

Smiling, Lindsey cuddled into his embrace. She needed to catch her breath. Ignoring the damp sheet beneath her, she drifted on the pleasant haze of post orgasmic high.

The squawk of a baby's cry had both of them tensing. Zadal pushed away and up first. Lindsey sat up beside him. They cocked their heads and waited for a secondary cry.

"Do you want me to comm Graeme?" Zadal asked, already reaching for the device at the side of the bed.

"No." Lindsey tossed aside the sheets and rose on a stretch. Her muscles were deliciously worked and limber. "I'll see to them. It's time for their feeding."

Zadal jumped from the bed and Lindsey snickered at his eagerness. "I'll clean up and join you."

Baruk and Zadal seemed to take an inordinate amount of delight from feeding their children. It gave Lindsey a much needed break from caring for triplets. His taut ass cheeks flexed as he dashed into her attached bathroom. Lindsey debated for all of a second then used the comm at the side of her bed. Graeme, to her pleasure, had his portable comm on and was already in the nursery tending to the little ones.

Which meant Lindsey could take a few extra minutes with her husband in their version of a shower.

Chapter 2

Baruk came home to a quiet house. The servants who maintained the estate had retired for the night and there was no one to greet him. Muffling a sigh of disappointment at being late again, he eased down the hall to Lindsey's room. He peered inside and knew immediately that it was empty.

The lavish furnishings he'd ordered long before selecting a wife or spouse partner fit his wife to a T. Expensive gowns decorated the bottom of the neatly made bed as well as the chair set next to a small table covered with books. Lindsey insisted on cleaning her room without help which meant the staff help was banned from her room. A decree Baruk didn't agree with but it wasn't worth arguing over.

He closed the door and came to Zadal's bedroom next. A quick glance inside showed his spouse partner sprawled in the massive bed. Without any clothing on. Grimacing, Baruk hurried by and stopped at the cracked door between Zadal's and his room. Graeme glanced up from his data pad at Baruk's entrance.

"Senate Leader Laars." The man bowed low.

"How are they?" Baruk didn't wait for an answer as he strode directly for the baby bed he'd had made to fit three newly born. The designer had been shocked then eager to commission a piece he would probably never get the opportunity to make again. Garulaxans did not have multiples. Lindsey continued to be more than Baruk could have dreamed time and again.

"They did well today. Sleeping longer at night. Finally."

"I have it from here." Baruk dismissed Graeme and leaned over the safety railing to pick up a tiny bundle. She mewled in his hold but as he cradled her close to his chest, she settled back with a purse of her pink lips.

Azalea. He held Azalea. Baruk laughed softly under his breath, distantly noting the door closing behind Graeme. Lindsey had Welsin, the clothing designer, stitch little initials in the girls clothing. None of them had mentioned it but it was hard to tell them apart because they were identical. After Lindsey had a minor breakdown days after the birth worried they would confuse the children and never know, it was Welsin's wife, Berline, who'd made the suggestion.

Baruk sat in one of the three overstuffed chairs placed together and leaned down to smell the baby sweet fragrance. He closed his eyes and once more thanked whatever powers that had led Lindsey to choose his world out of hundreds of others when she left Earth.

Their Triad may have had a rocky start but it was strengthened with the bonds of their love and the hurdles they'd overcome in the past.

Baruk rocked slowly then switched babies until he'd spent time with each one. It didn't matter that their blonde hair and blue eyes strongly suggested Zadal as the paternal donor for half their DNA. They were his daughters in heart and by Garulaxan law. Nothing could stem the love he had for them

Exhaustion dragged at Baruk by the time he commed for Graeme to return and sit with them through the night. He made his way to his bedroom and paused at the doorway.

A smile twitched Baruk's lips. He leaned a shoulder against the jamb and took a moment to marvel at the sight of his wife nestled into a mound of covers on his bed. It was a pretty safe guess she'd be in here. Lindsey did *not* believe in a day going by without spending the night with either Zadal or him at her side.

Her bedroom had become a room she mainly used to change clothes or shower. Sometimes he and Zadal would join her there but for the most part she ended in one of their beds. If it was a night of ménage as she called Triad marital sex, they'd all fall asleep in the same bed wherever that was.

She rolled to her side on a snuffle and the covers slipped down her shoulder, revealing the curve of a bare breast and furled nipple. Baruk inhaled and closed the door with his foot as he crossed the room to the bed.

Pregnancy had only enhanced her appeal to him. There were times Baruk feared he wouldn't get enough of Lindsey as she'd gotten more and more round with their children. Her lush figure had called to him in a way that left his cock hard from sun up to sun down. He was sure Zadal had taken note of his excessive attention.

Thankfully, his spouse partner hadn't taunted him about it. Much. Away from Lindsey there had been plenty of casual remarks.

'Lindsey looked extra tired this morning. Maybe let her sleep when she's in bed with you.'

'Is your goal to cause our wife to permanently limp?'

'Do you actually want the babies born with a bruise on their foreheads?'

Baruk snorted and undressed. His clothing was folded and put away with the same meticulous care he used with all of his things. He eased the sheets back and slid into his side of the bed. Lindsey immediately rolled toward him and wrapped an arm about his waist and threw a leg across his thighs.

Grinning, Baruk stretched an arm up behind his head and curved the other about her shoulders. The tension of the day faded away that easily as he closed his eyes.

"Rough day?"

Her soft inquiry snapped his eyes back open. Tipping his head to the side, Baruk met her drowsy gaze. "I thought you were asleep."

Her lips curled in a smile and she moved her arm higher to pat his cheeks. "I wanted to wait up for you. Make sure you're alright."

Because of his work schedule. She didn't have to say it but Baruk knew that was why. "I'm caught up now and should be able to do anything non-pressing from home now."

Lindsey snuggled into his side. The move pressed a full breast against his chest and a stiff nipple poked at him. His cock hardened. It had been several days since he'd last enjoyed his wife. Compared to the copious amount of time he had spent in bed with her while pregnant, he now had to balance his attention and share her with their girls.

Soft, even breaths fluttered along his throat. Disappointment welled. Of course she was tired and not interested in making love. Baruk closed his eyes with every intention of willing his cock to go down.

Soft fingers trailed across his chest, sending quivers down his spine. Baruk remained still as Lindsey continued to stroke her way down his torso, the dip of his belly and they paused below his waist. Waiting with his breath held, Baruk fought the urge to thrust his hips up.

"Are you tired?" she murmured.

Baruk groaned in relief and rolled to his side gathering her close. He buried one hand in her hair and the other between her legs. Even in the dark he caught her flinch and paused. "Lindsey?"

She caressed his face, her teeth a bright slash of white. "I'm okay. It's fine."

Baruk gentled his touch and slid one finger back and forth between her folds while his gaze stayed trained on her face. He didn't miss her wince and stopped immediately. "You're sore."

Once again, Baruk was annoyed at himself for not leaving work when Zadal had. The two of them had probably spent the evening together because Zadal had been working as much as Baruk and neither of them did well away from Lindsey for large stretches of time.

He eased his hand back, patted the curve of her waist and kissed the top of her head. "Get some rest."

The girls' sleep schedule had gotten better but despite having Graeme to help, he knew Lindsey pushed herself to do it all.

"I did. Earlier."

Before Baruk could respond, Lindsey broke from his hold and slid beneath the covers. His cock pulsed against his thigh in anticipation. She didn't make him wait long nor did she give him the slow build up she had perfected. Instead her mouth enveloped the head of his cock in one smooth swallow that had Baruk arching up.

He hissed out a breath and attempted to ease back but Lindsey planted her hands on his hips and pushed him to remain. He could have freed himself. She wasn't physically strong enough to restrain him but then her mouth began a lick sucking motion which had him on the verge of releasing.

"Slower, wife" he growled and reached down to thread his fingers through the blonde hair spread across his lap.

Lindsey's head continued to bob up and down but the pace she'd set eased some and Baruk allowed himself to relax against the bedding. Every few licks, her hands would run over his thighs, causing him to tense and jerk. On the third time he heard her snicker and Baruk found himself smiling as he stared at the ceiling.

Work troubles disappeared and true pleasure hummed through his veins as Baruk focused on Lindsey's mouth. The slick glide of her lips, the flick of her tongue and the moisture trickling down his length to pool on his groin.

Soon he was rocking back and forth, fingers tight in her hair as his orgasm roared closer.

"Yes, fuck. Yes, yes."

Lindsey moaned around his shaft and gripped the base tight as she sucked and hollowed her cheeks. The head of his cock went in and out as he watched until his breath became ragged. Sweat rolled into his eyes, blurring his vision of her blonde head. Humming, Lindsey cupped his sac with her free hand and pleasure slammed into him.

Baruk arched back, head pressed onto the pillow as he thrust upward and groaned. Lindsey didn't move until she'd drained every drop and Baruk collapsed into a boneless heap. His body shuddered as she adjusted the covers and crawled her way back up. He could barely move and bright flashes kept flickering over his gaze as she curled into him on the side.

"I love you," he managed when his heart ceased to race like an out of control hover-car.

"You, too." She kissed a spot on his chest.

***

Lindsey rested with her head propped on Baruk's chest, her hand directly over his heart. She smiled at the frantic beats against her fingers and breathed deeply of the slight musky scent to the air. Baruk ran his hand up and down her arm, drifting closer to her nipple with each pass.

When it came close again, Lindsey nipped his finger. "Stop. I'm fine."

She didn't need to find release since Zadal had taken very good care of her needs earlier. She'd only wanted to relax Baruk because she understood how much pressure he'd been under at work and because she loved connecting with both her husbands via sexual intimacy. Even if it was sometimes one sided. Though they never let her go to sleep without an orgasm from one or the other.

Baruk's breathing had settled into an even pattern when the comm by his bed buzzed. Lindsey leaned up carefully in order to not disturb Baruk. According to the color display on the buttons, it wasn't Graeme which meant the kids were fine. This was an external call. She was about to lay back down when thumps pounded on the door.

"Verat!" Baruk jerked upright, running a hand through his dark hair. He narrowed his gaze on the door when the pounding came again. "Enter."

"There's been an accident at one of the mines," Zadal stated as he hesitated in the doorway.

Lindsey sat up and rolled her eyes. Baruk didn't care if they ended up in her bed or Zadal's for the night but for some reason, Zadal was always reluctant about crossing into Baruk's bedroom domain. She was sure it had to do with the differences in their upbringing. After all, they lived in Baruk's billion square foot mansion on a stretch of land far beyond her ability to measure.

"Where? When?" Baruk was out of the bed in a flash and strode toward his bathroom without a care for his nudity.

Zadal came in and met Lindsey's stare. His tight expression eased some as he answered Baruk. "The alert came on my comm from Beline. I'm not sure which of your properties since its not possible to catalogue your full worth."

He said the last on a sarcastic note and Lindsey grinned. It was true Baruk came from a family of wealth and he'd gone on to create even more wealth. Beline was Zadal's first assistant and handled his business affairs while Aliya, his second assistant, handled his personal.

Water ran then Baruk strode back in still nude and entered his closet. Moments later he was dressed in perfectly tailored dark gray pants and a fitted gray sweater in a darker shade of gray that did all sorts of delicious things to Lindsey's middle. Welsin was the designer responsible for all of their clothing. After much complaining, Zadal had finally let Welsin create a new wardrobe befitting his high-level political and marital role. As evident by the sleek black on black outfit he currently wore.

"Is there anything I can do to help?" Lindsey finally asked as she searched the floor for the robe she'd worn to Baruk's bedroom.

"No." Baruk crossed to his comm as it sounded again. He paused to listen to whoever was on the other end then spoke. "Zadal has informed me. We're on our way."

Fuming, Lindsey raced from the room to her own and threw on a dress. She wished she still owned her jeans but the dress code on Garulax was antiquated in that women had to wear dresses. She dashed to the girls' room, startling Graeme awake in the bed added for him during overnight stays.

"Is everything alright, Lady Lindsey?" he asked.

It had taken a while but Lindsey accepted that marrying two Senate Leaders also gave her a fancy title. "Everything's fine but I'm leaving with Baruk and Zadal. There's been some sort of accident."

"I'll ask for help from the staff to watch over the girls."

Lindsey blew out a breath in relief. "I hate asking you to do more with them."

He grinned and waved her off as he settled back on the pillows. "For what Senate Baruk pays me, I don't do enough."

Lindsey's lips twitched as she dashed from the room with every intention of going with her husbands. She didn't see either in the hall and skipped down the spiral staircase to the lower level.

"Slow down before you break your neck," Zadal snapped as he gripped her arms when she reached the bottom.

Stair skipping was probably one of her favorite things about Baruk's house but it always did something to Zadal's nerves. Ignoring his familiar gripe, she eyed him and Baruk who stood at the door, impatience creasing his brows.

"I'm going with you. We can argue and delay whatever is going on or you can give in now."

Baruk snorted but he opened the door and waited. Zadal muttered under his breath but Lindsey didn't respond. One day he'd realize she wasn't a typical Garulaxan woman. She was from Earth and proud of it.

Chapter 3

They took one of Baruk's fancy vehicles and arrived at the site in one of the cities neighboring Teeve but more rural. Lindsey didn't venture out much since everything could be ordered and delivered. After her experience in being kidnapped, she wasn't overly fond of traveling away from the estate unless Baruk and Zadal were with her.

Activity and emergency crew hustled around, orders being called out and answered. As soon as he stopped, Baruk leaped out and was in the mix immediately. Zadal helped Lindsey out and guided her toward the three men Baruk had engaged in conversation. His hand was a secure weight on her lower back as she gazed at the harried expressions on those present.

The tension in the air was palpable. Flickering blue lights from the vehicles surrounding the area added a level of urgency to the scene. People rushed by and Lindsey only caught bits and pieces of what was said.

Collapse. Possible injuries. System failure.

"This is the only viable entry point," the dark-haired man in a reflective shirt said to Baruk, holding up a data pad as he pointed. "Over here is where the collapse occurred when the supporting beams gave way."

Brows pinched tight, Baruk leaned forward and pointed at something on screen. "Why didn't the emergency system alert at the first sign of integrity issues? This should have given an alarm long before the supports gave."

Lindsey missed most of the answer, distracted by the equipment rolling in their direction. Technology on Garulax was far superior to Earth so she wasn't surprised by the robo-machines with flashing yellow lights. Techs, she assumed, gathered around it with helmets shielding their heads and faces.

"That's not acceptable!" Baruk shouted, pulling her attention back.

Zadal stepped forward, nudging Lindsey's shoulder so she'd follow. When they were next to Baruk, Zadal asked, "What's the problem?"

Expression grim, Baruk snapped, "All of our mines are configured with advance alert systems. The moment any structural issues are detected, it should send an emergency alarm signaling techs to come out and inspect. On sites inspections are required before activity can resume if live personnel work in that section. Apparently, the Lead Supervisor assigned to this mine decided it wasn't worth having a tech come out and he signed off to reopen this segment noting the file as data error."

Steam practically billowed from his head as he flung his hand toward the entrance of the mine. "This should *not* have happened. We had these systems installed years ago for a reason. I don't tolerate danger to the workers who risk their lives with this job!"

And then Lindsey remembered. The anger and frustration wasn't simply because his people were at risk. Baruk had lost both his fathers in an accident at one of the mines the Laars family owned during a routine tour. Thirteen lives had been lost because the safety measures hadn't been sufficient when part of it had collapsed.

Zadal placed a calming hand on Baruk's shoulder. "Deal with the one responsible later. What can we do?"

Baruk's eyes flashed blue fire then he drew in a deep breath and exhaled. Remorse darkened his gaze as he faced the shadowed entrance of the mine. "This is the only entry point not impacted. The tunnel should lead to one of the center breezeways which branches off into several directions depending on what was being worked on. There's an evac point where workers would regroup in event an accident like this did occur and all preventative measures were bypassed."

"Good. Then it's a simple matter to go in and retrieve them."

The corner of Baruk's mouth curled. "Yes, a simple matter except no one here is familiar with this particular mine. The nearest employee is on route but he's an hour away."

Lindsey cleared her throat. She didn't know a lot about this but it would seem time was of the essence. When she thought of mines, she thought of antiquated underground caves more or less. "Do they have enough air to breathe?"

"The air system was compromised during the collapse." Baruk shoved a hand through his dark hair, the curls mussed and flying in every direction. He growled the next. "There are three men down there and only one personal breathing device because the same lead supervisor, who ignored the structural alert, took it upon himself to save likos by minimizing the number of devices based on how many individuals are on the team that work here."

Lindsey breath caught as she asked him to repeat himself. "How many devices do they have?"

Rage flashed as Baruk replied, "One."

"What about the supervisor? Wouldn't he need to be close since he's responsible for this location? He should be able to find the workers."

Zadal's question was a smart one but before Baruk could answer, a portly man stormed in their direction. His brown hair stood on end and his green tunic strained across his middle. He reached then, puffing out a breath, face flushed pink and sweat dotting his forehead.

"What is the meaning of this?"

"Lead Ronan Daris?" Baruk's voice was a dark growl.

Ronan nodded and pulled up the waist of his pants which drooped again as soon as he released them. "Yes. I'm in charge here. Why are you here? What's going on?"

Lindsey was stunned at his lack of awareness. Baruk's hands clenched at his sides. "I'm Baruk Laars, my family owns this mine."

Ronan's nostrils flared and his gaze narrowed. He swiped a hand through his unruly hair. "What brings you out and why was I summoned, Senator Leader Laars?"

"Did you not get the emergency communication?" Baruk asked with reasonable calm though Lindsey could tell he was anything but calm.

"Well, yes," he stuttered then bolstered his nerve by straightening his shoulders and standing tall.

Baruk's ire grew. "Then why are you just getting here?"

"These things happen and they tend to be false alarms. My assistant continued to comm, making a big deal so I decided to handle things. Be assured, Senate Leader, you can return home and I can handle everything."

Baruk lunged and Zadal caught him about the waist. Ronan squawked and stumbled back. "W-w-what is the meaning of this?"

Zadal was whispering adamantly in Baruk's ear. Ronan straightened and glared. "What is this about?"

"Because of you," Baruk snapped, "there are lives in danger."

Ronan stuttered and fear then bravado flashed across his features. "It has to be a mistake."

"We don't have time for this," Zadal cut in.

Lindsey was grateful he was with them. It was clear Baruk was running on pure emotion.

One of the workers standing with them spoke up. "We have extra breathing devices here someone can take down and then guide them out but none of us know where the evac point is. A wrong turn could delay the rescue attempt or trap another."

Ronan paled, blubbering his protest. "I can't go! I never learned the routes."

"Let me go, Zadal."

Lindsey shivered at the menace in Baruk's voice. Zadal carefully released Baruk, standing close in case he needed to intervene again.

"Are you saying you are not aware of the evac points for this location?"

Ronan gnawed his bottom lip. "I was supposed to memorize them as a condition of employment but never found the time. The safety measures here never fail. It's not an issue."

This time Zadal was prepared when Baruk's arm reached out. He caught Baruk's hand before he could grab Ronan.

"Get him out of here. He's pointless," Zadal said over his shoulder as he blocked Baruk's access to wreak havoc on Ronan.

There was a minor scuffle and Ronan complained the entire time as he was dragged away. The original three who had been in conversation with Baruk huddled close. "We're sorry, Senate Leader. He's been like this since he started a few months ago. One of us should have reported him and didn't."

"What's your name?" Baruk asked in a much calmer voice. "Cadd."

Baruk tugged at his shirt and smoothed his clothes out. "I know where it is, Cadd. I can go in with the devices and find them."

Of course Baruk would know but that didn't stop Lindsey's protest. "You can't go in there."

Baruk faced Cadd and the two others. "Give me a moment with my spouse partner and wife."

They glanced at Lindsey with sympathetic looks and faded back some distance. Lindsey swallowed and tried to think of a way to stall Baruk from risking himself. Zadal folded his arms over his chest. "If you're going in, then so am I."

Baruk snorted and matched him glare for glare. "One of us needs to stay out here with our wife."

"All the more reason I should go in and you stay out here after telling me where to go." Zadal's brows lowered as he made the announcement.

"That makes no sense. It's easier for me to go. You don't know anything about these mines, Zadal."

A blond brow arched up as Zadal responded, "You're too emotional and connected, Baruk. Your decision making is compromised by this situation."

There was a pause and the two stared at one another without speaking.

Baruk broke the stare off. "If something were to happen, Lindsey—"

"Then we both go." Zadal's gaze was unrelenting. "Think of it as your chance to finally get me to follow where you lead, Baruk."

Lindsey's heart picked up its pace at the thought of both her husbands going inside a potential death trap. Then she thought of the ones trapped inside. What if they had spouses worried about them? Could she put Baruk and Zadal's lives ahead of them if Baruk really could get them out?

"Can't someone else go in?" Lindsey asked.

"No." Baruk gripped the back of his neck. Fury blasted from his gaze though not directed at her. "There's not enough time to wait for experts who know these mines the way I do. This is on my family. We assure the families that all safety measures are taken at every property we own."

Lindsey rubbed his arm and made soothing noises. Zadal shifted beside her. "We're wasting time, Baruk. I'm going with you. We'll also have two emergency workers accompany us."

Indecision crossed Baruk's face. "It's too dangerous. The risk—"

Lindsey slashed her hand through the air. "No. If it's too dangerous for them, it's too dangerous for anyone."

"Zadal doesn't belong in there!" Baruk roared.

Lindsey caught Zadal's flinch before he masked his expression. "Actually, because of the marriage agreement, I'm fairly certain this property is one of the ones you added my name to."

Because Baruk had generously given a portion of his fortune to Zadal without his knowledge at the time of their Triad.

Baruk snorted and dropped his hand to his side. "Of all the times to remember which properties you own or are a part of, you choose now?"

Zadal shrugged but Lindsey wasn't fooled by the bland look in his brown eyes. Baruk's words had hurt him for some reason.

"One of us needs to stay for Lindsey. Why risk both of us?" Baruk attempted a conciliatory tone.

"I don't want either of you in there. BUT—" she held up a hand before they could interrupt and stared hard at Baruk. "the only way you're going in there is if you take someone with you. It can be Zadal or someone else but you will not risk your life by yourself out of some misplaced guilt for the actions of another."

Zadal smirked. "We need to hurry, Baruk. Save the martyrdom for work."

Lindsey knew they'd won when Baruk sighed and signaled the three guys to come back over. "You're right."

Rubbing at the pimpled flesh on her arms, Lindsey watched carefully as Baruk and Zadal were fitted with black matte safety suits and handed the breathing apparatus to give the men inside. They also received special helmets with a front shielding panel.

"The map of the inner paths and sections are on here but nothing's marked." Cadd, the man who seemed to be in charge gave Baruk a silver wristlet with a wide band to match his own band.

Baruk snapped it on his left wrist. "I'll find them. I know where the evac space is for each of the mines owned by my family."

"Remember," another added, "the air supply inside is good for another forty-five minutes. At that point, they will have to either start sharing the one personal breathing device available or attempt to come out."

Baruk glanced at the wrist unit. "Right now the indicator shows they're not moving which is smart. Has anyone been able to get in contact with them or let them know help is on the way?"

Cadd's lips pressed tight and it wasn't hard to sense his frustration. "Communication went down with everything else but the site tech is here and will keep trying to get it back up."

"Then we move. You and another are with me and my spouse partner."

Rushing off, Cadd approached one of the team and began an intense conversation.

Holding his helmet under his arm, Baruk approached Lindsey and cupped her face with his free hand. "Will you be alright waiting here?"

Tears burned but Lindsey blinked them back and nodded. "Just be careful."

Zadal joined them, his body large and intimidating in the gear. Blond hair ruffled and brown eyes clear, he was the image of a strong warrior come to life. Lindsey sniffed and scrubbed at her cheek when a few tears spilled over. Zadal frowned. "If you cry now, what will you do when we come out?"

She released a watery chuckle and smacked his chest. "As long as you come out."

Baruk smoothed his thumb across her cheek and leaned forward to kiss her brow. "We'll be back shortly."

He slid his helmet on and waited for Zadal to do the same. Her taciturn husband dropped his helmet on the ground instead and grasped Lindsey at the waist. She gasped and braced her hands on his shoulders for support. His kiss on her mouth was long and deep. When he eased up, he stayed close enough every breath wisped against her lips. "I love you."

"Love you back." Lindsey cupped his face. She stared into his eyes. There were so many things she wanted to say but nothing was going to happen to him so she pushed them back and only said in a husky whisper, "Watch, Baruk. His fathers died in a similar accident."

Zadal pressed his lips tight then nodded and stepped back. He bent to grab his helmet and then he and Baruk walked away with the pack containing the breathing devices slung over Baruk's shoulder. Two men in matching safety suits joined them at the entrance and all four disappeared inside. Lindsey's heart stuttered when she could no longer see their tall forms.

"Would you like to listen in?"

She spun at the voice to her left. Beside her stood a red-haired man holding a small black wire with a hook on the end. "Excuse me?"

She understood several of the languages and dialects spoken on Garulax since she couldn't have an actual translator implanted but wanted to make sure she understood what he was asking.

"I'm Tamlin, part of the first crew to arrive. This is the mic which will let the team out here listen to them in case they need help or run into any trouble."

Relief poured through Lindsey and she eagerly accepted it. The curved portion slid behind her ear easily and the thin wire extended along her jaw.

"I have you on mute for when they activate it," he added with a grin and thumbs up before sauntering away.

***

As soon as they crossed the threshold of the mine entrance, the worker next to Cadd tapped the side of his helmet. "Turning on audio to the crews outside and switching to air supply."

"Activating," Cadd said, mimicking the steps.

Baruk did the same and confirmed with a nod when Zadal did his. Once they went below, there would be no breathable air.

"We have all four of you on live," someone from the outside responded.

The sound was crisp and clear in Baruk's ear which meant the others heard it as well.

"You didn't have to come," Baruk muttered to Zadal when they were out of earshot of the others.

His voice was muffled and distorted due to the helmets they wore but Zadal heard him clear enough. He snorted. "I had the feeling you would need my rational approach to situations as your own may be skewed by the past."

Baruk's shoulders stiffened but he didn't slow or turn to face Zadal. They were moving through the twisting, dark tunnels at a pace faster than a walk but slower than an all out run. Baruk only glanced at the digital map displayed on the wrist unit about his arm once. He really did have the layout of this particular mine mapped out in his memory.

Every breath Zadal took echoed within his helmet. His vision never fogged and the face shield remained clear giving him an impressive view of the mine. If he didn't know he was underground, he'd believe he was in a high tech lab facility.

Shoulders hunched, their group squeezed through narrow spaces wide enough for one at a time and slogged through ankle high water flowing from the walls. At least, the hard surface of the flooring was solid beneath their shoes.

"I take it this isn't normal?" Zadal asked when Baruk didn't respond to his earlier taunt.

Baruk's helmeted head shook in the negative, his face glowing briefly from the dim light mounted on the helmet. "There's a leak in the pipes imbedded through the walls. The integrity has been compromised causing this."

The walls themselves were pearly white, a sheen reflecting the substance coating it to keep the interior cool in the warmer clime and warm during the colder temps. Recessed lighting in the ceiling kept the space bright instead of the dark one would expect for an underground work site.

Then the lights flickered.

Zadal glanced at Baruk who signaled to Cadd and the other worker with them to keep moving. "Its running off of power from the emergency system activated by the collapse while the main power has been shut down and rerouted."

Cadd spoke up to be heard over the intermittent alarm beeping from above. "The life beacons are solid green so we know those trapped down here are still alive."

For now. Zadal didn't want to be grim but it was very likely that the workers down here might not make it out. He glanced around. The likelihood of all of them getting out was a concerning factor as well.

They came to the end of a tunnel and faced a ladder built into the wall. Zadal looked to Baruk for direction, trusting him over the men he didn't know.

"Up through the hatch. There's a hall that will lead to a security access panel. It's behind a sealed door accessible with a specific code."

Considering they'd spent almost fifteen of the forty-five minutes and would have to travel the same distance back, they needed to hurry. Cadd stepped forward and grasped the rails. "I'll go first, Senate Leaders."

Baruk followed and Zadal waved at the last guy then brought up the rear. Cadd shoved a removable section of the ceiling aside, creating an opening to go through. Zadal made sure to not close it behind them.

"Hurry," Baruk said, taking the lead once more.

Their pace picked up to a trot, boots thundering and echoing off of the walls. The lights continued their eerie dance, winking in and out. Zadal held his breath, waiting for when they would completely give out. Baruk smirked in his direction. "Afraid of the dark?"

Zadal muttered a curse under his breath which caused Baruk to chuckle. Based on what Lindsey told him right before he left, Zadal hoped their typical bickering would alleviate some of the stress creasing Baruk's face.

Chapter 4

Baruk kept his breath calm and steady. He was an expert at presenting a calm façade on the outside. Internally, he was fairly certain his nerves were strung tight. The late night comm followed by the news of an incident at one of his property would have usually caused a modicum of worry. The fact the incident occurred at a mine and actual workers were trapped inside shifted it into something far more complex.

Everything about this was an emotional storm he struggled to battle through yet he couldn't stand back and let others with no knowledge of the location step in. That would have been akin to creating a greater failure and he already shouldered the bulk of the blame for not realizing that lead supervisor Ronan was incompetent before this disaster occurred. Whatever happened here, he was ultimately at fault.

"Wait!" Baruk held up a hand for everyone to stop. He studied the walls and compared it to the mental map he recalled and the diagram on the wrist unit. A glance to the right assured he was in the correct space. Baruk pointed toward a seemingly empty room. "In here."

"This is just a utility back up," Cadd said, his tone puzzled.

"Only in appearance."

It was designed that way in case of various scenarios. He and his mother had gone over everything with a certified structural team when redoing all of the mines their family owned. She'd also contacted Baruk's best friend, Ruin, and gained their family's agreement to upgrade the safety measures at their facilities as well.

Sofia Laars hadn't wanted anyone else to suffer as she had when she'd lost both of her husbands in an incident during a routine tour. She'd raised him and his sister with a strong hand, guiding influence and above all compassion toward anyone who worked for them. Wealth came with privilege and they tried to wield it wisely.

Inside of the room, Baruk went directly toward the main wall and pressed along the center, fingers searching for a familiar bump. Once he made contact, a small panel opened. The others crowded around him. A holo-screen and keyboard took up most of the space inside the panel.

"Are you sure your code will work?" Cadd asked.

Baruk nodded as he entered the long sequence of numbers. His family had an override for almost everything and it was updated annually. A series of clicks and a whoosh signaled a release of pressure as a door across the room swung open.

"Where does this lead?" Zadal asked, peering inside the dark interior with the others.

"It will take us underground and get us to the other side since the damage so far is limited to top side." Baruk hefted the pack carrying the breathing devices higher on his shoulder and hoped the workers inside were well enough to make it out under their own strength. If not, this task would get exponentially more difficult.

There were a dozen stairs to descend into the underground tunnels. Once they reached the bottom, water ceased to drip and run about their feet. The emergency lights gave off a green glare which reflected off of their helmets. Baruk kept to the front and led the way. The group stayed on his heels, the air vibrating with fear and worry at what they'd find.

They were almost to the evac point and Baruk had a moment to hope he wasn't mistaken in assuming that those who worked here would be aware of the emergency procedures. What if Ronan had ignored other mandatory training? He shook off the negative thoughts and said a brief prayer.

They reached the final door designated with a large red X within a red circle. This was the evac point. As Baruk entered another string of numbers on the keypad to the right of the handle, sweat trickled down his temple. His heart rate sped up, fingers trembling when he entered the final number.

The door squeaked then popped open. They all jumped back. Cadd gripped Baruk's arm. "Allow me, Senate Leader."

Not wanting to waste time, Baruk gave in. Zadal crowded at his side. One by one they entered the sparse room and relief hit Baruk hard. Seated on the floor wearing expressions of hope, were the three mine workers.

Baruk's breath escaped on a shudder and his knees weakened. Zadal squeezed his shoulder and Baruk accepted the support. As much as they bothered one another personally, they stood side by side publicly.

He rushed forward to access the state of the closest man. Silver streaked his dark hair and lines etched the corners of his eyes.

"I'm Baruk Laars. My family owns this facility and we're here to help you out."

"I'm Janz, Senate Leader Laars. Thank you for coming."

"Survivors found," Cadd reported as he kneeled next to one of the men.

Cheers erupted in Baruk's ears and he found himself smiling also.

"We have roughly twenty minutes to get out of here," Zadal reminded as he helped a worker to stand.

"Is anyone badly injured?" Baruk asked, watching Cadd and his partner manage the last worker between them.

Negative head shakes. Their clothes were dirty but they seemed aware and cognizant which meant the air supply hadn't reached critical levels yet.

Baruk shrugged the pack off of his shoulder and opened it to retrieve the breathing devices and handed them out. "Let's get these on. We'll have to rush on the way out. No delays."

The devices would last only as long as the allotted time on the gauges.

"I'm glad you all found safety and waited," Baruk added as he helped Janz notch the straps of the breathing device about his head and settled the mask on the lower half of his face.

Janz took a couple of test breaths and grinned. Baruk's shoulders eased slightly as he eyed the two approaching him with their devices already in place. He stood and kept an arm about Janz until he seemed to find his balance.

"I'm Garwin and this is my brother Cabe." Garwin patted Baruk's back. "Thank you. Thank you for coming. We didn't think we'd make it."

The device over the lower half of his face made Garwin's voice deep and raspy. Baruk accepted the thanks and activated his mic. "Four workers and four on the rescue team coming out."

"Understood. Is medical care required?"

Baruk eyed everyone once more. "None needed."

"Rescue team, you have eighteen minutes of air."

"On our way," Baruk responded. "Cadd, can you remember the way out?"

"As long as I don't have to enter the fancy codes."

Baruk laughed. "Take the lead and don't slow down for anything."

It was going to be a lot easier going out knowing the men had survived. What had started as a reminder of one of the worst days of his life was ending on an upbeat note.

"Good job, Baruk. For once, you were not in need of my guidance."

Baruk glanced at his spouse partner. Zadal arched a brow in his direction and Baruk couldn't resist his sarcastic quip. "The day I need your guidance is the day the High Councilor should replace me."

They headed back the way they'd come and Zadal's laughter flowed behind him. Biting back a grin, Baruk kept to the jogging pace as they retraced their steps. They reached the latch leading to the ladder down. Baruk stepped aside after gazing down the opening to make sure everything continued to look clear. The water on the floor was still negligible.

A yellow light blinked on the face shield of his helmet. *Warning. Air supply low.*

Cursing came from everyone who'd received a similar alert on their helmets. Baruk gestured at the ladder. "Go down, stick together. At this point, run. It's straight from here back to the entrance."

***

Zadal waited as the two rescue team members went down the ladder first. Next the three mine workers gripped the opening then hopped down. Zadal prepared to follow Baruk and bring up the rear.

"See you on the bottom," Baruk said, flicking his fingers in a casual salute toward Zadal.

Zadal's lips quirked. He'd witness the relief on Baruk's face when they'd found the workers. If this had ended in the other direction, it would have been difficult for his friend and spouse partner to recover. Zadal joked about Baruk's wealth often but his level of compassion was greater than many Zadal had come into contact with daily.

Baruk hopped through the opening, his hands on the rails. His lips parted, no doubt to taunt Zadal again. The ceiling gave an ominous rumble. They both glanced up. A loud crack resounded.

"Zadal!"

Zadal jumped back as the floor shook and rolled beneath him. Losing his balance, he dropped to one knee and yelled to Baruk. "Go! Get out of here!"

One of them needed to get back to Lindsey. Zadal planted both hands on the ground and pushed upright. The walls and floor continued to rock and shake, flinging Zadal back into a wall. His face shield cracked as he slid down, hitting his elbow hard. Shooting pain raced up his arm. Jagged lines appeared in the walls and the lights popped and sizzled.

"Get up, Zadal!"

"I'm coming. Move back."

"Fuck! You better be right behind me." Zadal had one last glance of Baruk's wide eyes before his head ducked from view.

Heart in his throat, Zadal lunged forward. The lid of the opening slammed close with a solid thunk before he reached it. Shards of fear pierced Zadal's chest. He crawled forward and ripped at the handle. It snapped off from his brutal grip. Frantic, he pried at the edges only to slice the skin on his fingertips. Zadal slumped on his haunches.

Mouth dry, he stared in horror at his only means of exit being closed off.

Warning. Air supply low.

***

Lindsey received the announcement when everyone else did and found herself giddy with relief. Listening to Baruk's voice provided reassurance that he and Zadal were okay. She glanced around at the crew cheering and slapping each others' backs. This was a celebratory time. No one had died despite the incompetence of the one in charge.

She glared at Ronan who remained on site. Every now and then he tried to give orders but with Baruk's presence here, no one was paying him any attention. Lindsey twisted her fingers together and rose up on her toes, searching the entrance. Shortly, everyone would come through and they could go home. She wanted to hug her babies tight and sleep curled in the arms of husbands tonight.

Wrapping her arms about her torso, she rocked from side to side, not sure why the hair at her nape curled or why she suddenly had the desire to run toward the mine screaming. Tamlin came over, eyes bright. The festive air had everyone on a high for good reason.

"Did you hear?"

Lindsey nodded.

"It won't be long," he continued as if seeking to comfort her with his words.

Did her face reveal the fear suddenly coursing through her veins? She tried to smile but her lips quivered. Her stomach knotted and for a brief moment, Lindsey worried she'd throw up.

"Do you need to sit, Lady Lindsey?"

Waving her hand at his concern, Lindsay paced away. What was wrong with her? Maybe she needed to check on the girls.

"Rescue team, you have eighteen minutes of air."

Lindsey jolted. She pressed her fingers to the earpiece she wore.

"On our way."

That was Baruk. Lindsey exhaled to calm her rampaging pulse. They were okay. Everyone was okay. As much as Lindsey repeated the words, it didn't help. Her skin wanted to burst and she actually gripped her hands hard enough to leave imprints from her nails on her palms.

The ground suddenly heaved, drawing Lindsey's gaze toward the mine. Thunderous booms filled the air. Shouts, orders were called out but Lindsey couldn't look away from the entrance.

"Emergency power is out!" Someone yelled.

"Please, Baruk. Zadal. Come back to me," she whispered under her breath and tried to ignore the burn in her chest.

Chapter 5

"Zadal!" Baruk stared as the panel slammed closed.

Cadd and the group hesitated but Baruk yelled, "Keep going. Get everyone out!"

"Senate Leader—"

"Go!" he roared and they raced off.

The lights above went out but the swish of water from their feet let him know they were leaving. Baruk felt his way around the groove until he found the handle. The entire structure chose that moment to rattle violently. He paused, holding tight to the rungs of the ladder and braced his weight.

As soon as it settled, Baruk reached back up. Giving the latch a rough twist, he pushed at the panel. Behind him a hiss and pop sounded. Baruk didn't need to turn to know a pipe had burst and water was rushing in. This was bad. Baruk climbed up and came face to face with Zadal.

Darkness surrounded them but the light on their helmets illuminated their faces in an eerie glow.

"Now I owe you," were the first words from Zadal's mouth.

Baruk snorted, not realizing how grateful he was to hear the familiar snark. "Not yet. We can't go that way now."

Zadal froze as he stood beside Baruk. "What do you mean?"

"Exactly what I said." Baruk closed the opening. "The integrity continues to degrade and the pipes below burst filling the halls with water. There's no way we will make it out that way."

"Lindsey is going to kill us," Zadal said in such a manner Baruk barked out an unexpected laugh.

"Rescue team, advise as to status."

Cadd's voice snapped, "We see the entrance. Senate Leader Laars stayed behind. Senate Leader Gatar was trapped in one of the tunnels."

"Senate Leaders, advise as to status."

Baruk activated his mic and tried to respond. Scratchy connection. Then more static. "I can't get through. See if you can."

Zadal shook his head. "Nothing."

They'd lost their connection to the emergency and rescue crews on the outside.

"There's another way out but it won't be easy."

"We die here or we die trying to get out," Zadal quipped.

Unfortunately, it would be exactly like that because they were running out of air. Baruk didn't need the flickering yellow light on his screen to remind him. "Let's go. No one's dying today. "

Not if he could help it.

***

"Senate Leaders, advise as to status."

Lindsey waited for a response from Baruk or Zadal. The silence was unnerving. Five men came rushing from the entrance. Hair matted and clothes torn, it was easy to recognize the workers who had been trapped. The two rescuers who had accompanied Baruk and Zadal ripped the helmets from their heads and gasped for breath as they dropped to the ground. She hurried toward them along with several others.

"The Senate Leaders," Cadd managed before coughing. "The mine is still unstable. The whole area flooded. They're trapped."

Lindsey bit down on her knuckles, holding in a cry. Gazes turned in her direction. She straightened. "I'm not leaving. I am staying here until my husbands walk out of that mine."

The wait was interminable. Lindsey ran her hands through her hair repeatedly. It probably resembled a rat's nest. She didn't care.

"How long?" she asked Cadd and Tamlin. Both had chosen to wait by her side.

Crews had managed to get the emergency power back up but there was nothing they could do about the air.

"Ten minutes," Cadd said after checking the wrist band he still wore.

Ten minutes of air. Ten minutes to learn how fate would deal with her. Lindsey heaved a shaky breath. Suddenly static crackled in the ear piece. "Alternate...ex-it...t-t-there...soon."

Baruk! Lindsey recognized his voice. Tears burned and her throat swelled as she tried to swallow beyond the lump. Did that mean he was alright? What about Zadal? Dizziness swamped her senses and Lindsey stumbled. Tamlin, or was it Cadd? One of them steadied her with a hand to her back.

***

They had lights again. Baruk kept checking the unit on his wrist. Zadal pressed a hand to the twinge in his side. Running flat out in dim lighting wasn't the smartest thing he'd ever done. Baruk didn't leave him much choice though. His spouse partner was adamant they were getting out alive.

Zadal had his doubts. Lindsey would be devastated. He thought of his daughters. Never seeing them grow up. His vision grew hazy, causing his steps to wobble. Zadal put up a hand to the wall and staggered. Chest tight, he drew in a deep breath and coughed.

"Zadal." Baruk tugged on his forearm.

Zadal pursed his lips. His fingers tingled and his tongue felt numb. "Som...someth...not right."

"You shouldn't be feeling the effects yet." Baruk shifted in front of him, his hands gripping the sides of Zadal's helmet to lift his sagging head.

Why was it so hard to keep his head up?

"*Verat*! The shield is splintered. You're losing air faster than me."

Well that explained a lot. Zadal leaned away. "Keep going. Don't leave Lindsey alone."

There was no way he'd make it. Zadal wanted to laugh. He'd finally believed he deserved the good in his life. Foolish. There was no good for a *briot* and son of a sex worker.

"Neither of us is leaving her. Snap out of it, Zadal. We go together, or we both die because I'm not leaving you."

Zadal hadn't expected such a vehement response. Another deep inhale and he shook off the fuzzy thoughts clouding his mind. "Right."

He allowed Baruk to lead him, doing his best to stay upright. It became a matter of placing one foot in front of the other. They ran in an odd tangle of limbs as Baruk kept them upright and looped an arm about Zadal's waist. It was a race against time at this point.

"How much air?" he asked Baruk since his own counter was damaged by the cracks to his helmet.

"Three minutes," Baruk huffed as they skidded to a stop at a steel door. There were beams from the ceiling blocking it. Baruk propped him against the wall opposite the door. "Don't die."

Breathing unsteady, Zadal blinked away the dots floating in front of his eyes. His chest was on fire and every inhale sent slices of pain through him. "Couldn't the miners have left this way?"

"No air. They never would have survived without the personal breathing devices." Baruk didn't turn as he gave the sharp response. He shoved at the beams and bits obstructing the door only to reveal the mangled handle. "Nothing is ever easy."

Warning. Air supply critical.

"Baruk." Zadal needed to let him know it was over. "Baruk. Listen to me."

His spouse partner paused, chest heaving and turned to face him. "What?!"

Zadal blinked as the walls of the room spun around him. He wasn't sure how he found the energy but his mouth ticked up in the corner. "It's over for me."

"Shut up. Beyond this door is the outside."

"Take care of the girls," Zadal slurred and slid to the floor. "Love Lindsey."

Baruk turned away and kicked at the door. Over and over, the loud bangs echoing around him. The yellow light on

Zadal's screen changed to red. He tore the helmet from his head, gasping. No air. Couldn't breathe.

"Zadal, no!"

Zadal closed his eyes and never felt the floor make contact with his face.

Chapter 6

When Zadal crashed to the floor, Baruk's chest constricted. He put everything he had into the next kick and the door flew open, sagging from the hinges. Racing to Zadal, he kneeled next to his friend and placed his hand at his throat. The pulse was erratic. Baruk slid his arms under Zadal's back and legs.

"Heavy fucker." Groaning, he surged to his feet, the weight almost sending him back to the floor. Baruk gritted his teeth and walked.

Warning. Air supply low.

He wouldn't quit. There was no way they reached the exit for it to end like this. One foot in front of the other, Baruk pressed on. He kept walking as he grew light headed. Kept walking as his vision became hazy.

Baruk focused on the end goal. Lindsey and their kids. And Zadal. His spouse partner wasn't just a work peer. They were friends. Both of them were coming through this alive. "Don't die on me, Zadal. I promise to haunt you in this life and the next."

No response. Not that he expected one. He pushed forward, dragging air into his lungs. Wouldn't quit. Couldn't. Light shone ahead and Baruk knew he was close. He just had to walk across the threshold to the outside and medics would take care of Zadal.

One foot then the next. Speed was foregone for accuracy. As long as he stayed upright and kept moving, he would make it.

Warning. Air supply critical.

Baruk didn't have a spare hand to take the helmet from his head. He didn't care. With every staggering step, he wheezed desperate for air. Vision foggy, sound reached him. Voices. One foot in front of the other. Bright lights singed his pupils.

Shouts. Baruk couldn't make sense of anything.

***

"They're coming! I see them!"

Lindsey's heart leaped. She ran with the swell of the crowd toward the other side of the mine. The sight that greeted her stopped Lindsey in her tracks. She wanted to scream but couldn't. Baruk staggered out, carrying Zadal in his arms. Her husband was limp, disheveled hair covering his face.

"Zadal!" She drew near, tears streaming.

Baruk fell to his knees but continued to clutch Zadal tight to his chest. Medical personnel surrounded them and Lindsey had to shove her way through.

"Baruk! Zadal!"

Someone held a clear mask over Zadal's face. Baruk's helmet was tossed aside and a similar mask was placed over his face as he was lowered to a sitting position. Lindsey slid to her knees between them.

Confusion glittered in Baruk's gaze. "Zadal?"

Lindsey gripped Baruk's hand. "You brought him out."

He nodded then slumped backward to the ground. Medics kneeled around them and smiled in Lindsey's direction. "We have them. Everything's fine, Lady Lindsey."

More than fine because she had both of her husbands. Cadd and Tamlin squeezed her shoulders. "Your husbands are good men, Lady Lindsey."

She accepted more accolades on behalf of Zadal and Baruk. The rescued miners were next. Effusive thanks she didn't know how to deal with. The medics deemed their conditions warranted a trip to the medical center for supervised care. They were taken to the largest one in the city of Teeve where Baruk and Zadal were kept in observation overnight. The next morning they were released. Groggy and still out of it, Zadal and Baruk had each sought their own bedroom, falling back to sleep.

Lindsey was grateful to be home. She stopped in the nursery. Graeme had kept her updated during the night. Her daughters had slept through all of the excitement.

"I'm sorry to have left you with them," she murmured, not wanting to wake her darlings.

Graeme stretched his arms above his head. "It is always a pleasure to be with them. They never made a peep."

"Do you want me to take over?" Lindsey was exhausted but she never wanted Graeme to feel as if she used him.

He chuckled and shook his head. "I think you're almost asleep on your feet. Two of the house servants are coming to take over and I'll have the morning meal then return to watch them until you and the Senate Leaders are up."

"Are you sure?"

"Yes." He nudged her toward the door.

Lindsey tugged at tiny toes and rubbed the blonde fuzz on their heads before seeking her own bed for rest.

It was the shouting that woke her later. Lindsey stretched in her bed and yawned.

"You risked your life for nothing!"

"I should have known I'd get no thanks."

Baruk and Zadal were arguing outside her bedroom door. Lindsey threw on a robe and hurried into the hall. Both stood glaring at one another. Shirtless and hair mussed, Zadal had his fists clenched, shooting daggers at Baruk.

Her dark-haired husband wore a tailored high collared jacket and matching pants in black. Behind him, his first and second assistants hovered. Lindsey dismissed them with a head jerk. Kimsha and Mala scurried off.

Lindsey folded her arms over her chest and tapped her foot until they noticed her presence. Brown and blue eyes widened. She pointed a finger before either could approach. "Last night was the scariest outside of my being sold as a sex slave and going on the run. Today, I want to enjoy the fact my husbands are still alive but instead, I woke to you fighting."

Remorse glimmered in Baruk's gaze and Zadal had the grace to look sheepish. Baruk eased over to her and drew her into his embrace. Lindsey dropped her arms and held him tight. All of the fear and worry from the night before rolled through her. "I'm sorry, wife."

"I was scared," she said on a sniffle. "I don't want to lose either of you."

Zadal came up behind her, his chest a firm weight against her back. "If Baruk had not been stubborn, you would have at least had one husband survive."

Lindsey stiffened and broke away to face Zadal. "Are you serious?"

What was on his mind lately? Did he not realize how important he was?

Shrugging, Zadal wiped a hand down his face. "I'm only saying that—"

"I'm more important," Baruk finished for him.

Zadal glared and sensing another shouting match, Lindsey held up a hand. "What do you mean?"

Zadal's jaw locked. Baruk had no qualms about answering. "Zadal is mad that I didn't leave him. He continues to doubt his place in this Triad."

Lindsey's heart lurched. She touched Zadal's chest. "Is that true?"

"Baruk is the more worthy husband in this relationship, Lindsey."

"I love you. Both of you. Equally. I would not have been okay if you hadn't come out of that mine alive, Zadal. I can't believe you thought otherwise." For effect, she deliberately squeezed a few tears out.

Zadal paled. His mouth opened and closed then he awkwardly patted her back. "I'm sorry. Don't cry."

She added a sob and covered her face with both hands. Zadal pulled her into a hug. Over his shoulder, Baruk quirked a brow. Lindsey winked.

"I want to be close to you. I need to feel my husbands are alive."

"Whatever you want, Lindsey." Zadal lifted her and carried her into her bedroom.

When he gently lowered her to the tousled sheets, Lindsey curled her fingers toward Baruk. He stopped beside her bed and opened the buttons of his jacket. She shivered as more and more of his chest was bared with each twist of his fingers. Zadal simply tugged at the loose fitting pants and stepped out of them. His eager cock twitched once free. The throbbing length bumped his thigh as he climbed onto the bed to join her.

Lindsey reached out and smoothed her hand in a firm stroke up and down the rigid shaft. Flushed a vibrant red, the head thrust passed the folds. Moisture filled her mouth as Zadal kneeled next to her while she pumped her fist over his cock.

Zadal gazed down at her, a bemused expression on his face. "I never tire of watching you touch me."

Lindsey trembled, her thighs spreading of their own accord as Baruk came into the bed on the opposite end. She settled on her back, her hand continuing its even pace while she relished being surrounded on both sides by her husbands. Everything would be perfect if only Zadal would accept that she loved him as deeply as she loved Baruk.

Baruk threaded his fingers in her hair, turning her face toward him. Up close, the strain in his eyes was clear. His lips traced over her cheek, her nose then hovered at her temple. His words were whisper light when he spoke. "You're exactly what he needs."

She wanted to respond, to ask him how he knew what thoughts ran through her head. Baruk took the option away when his mouth landed on hers with fierce intensity. Her lips parted and his tongue swept inside. She loosened her hold on Zadal's cock and rolled on her side, partially facing Baruk. Zadal eased down behind her, his body a warm presence.

Shivers rolled down her spine. His breath stirred the hair at the back of her neck. His tongue teased the sensitive curve as

Baruk cupped her breasts and squeezed. Lindsey tried to gasp and he deepened the kiss until she was spinning out of control. Zadal slid his palm over her butt, caressed her hip then glided around her inner thigh. Lindsey lifted her leg to rest around Baruk.

He groaned and ended the kiss. Lips moist, he said, "Relax. Let us take care of you like you take care of us."

Lindsey could only nod. She was wet and growing wetter by the second. Zadal's questing hand covered her mound, his fingers parting her folds with ease. She moaned and rocked against Baruk. His gaze smoldered as he lowered it and pinched her nipples. The arc of pain had Lindsey tensing then the swell of pleasure followed. She spread her leg higher up Baruk's waist in an effort to get closer.

Zadal mouthed the curve of her shoulder, nipping kisses and soft licks of his tongue. Lindsey wanted more and twisted her neck to the side for more. His lips moved and she sensed his smile as he rubbed between her legs, fingers finding the swollen bump between her slit. Lindsey jerked and Zadal's chuckle rasped against her flesh. "Responsive to every touch."

She was overloaded. With Baruk fondling her breasts in rhythmic pumps and flicking her nipples, it was hard to concentrate. Add in Zadal's working hand in her most intimate place and she was close to coming.

"Front or back?" Baruk asked.

Lindsey frowned, wondering what he meant.

"I think I want to sink into her wet heat and drown in her pleasure."

Zadal. He was talking to Zadal. With practiced moves, they switched places. Zadal rested on his back and eased

Lindsey atop him. She bent her knees and straddled her fair-haired husband. Baruk shifted behind her, his hands on her butt as he grasped tight. She planted her hands by the pillow and arched as he came in close, hard cock nestled between her cheeks.

"I think we're all in the mood for something fast and hard," Zadal murmured as he looked up at her.

She was soaked and quivering on the edge of climax. Each time she had both of them in bed with her, Lindsey's body craved the release only they could give.

"Lift up," Baruk coached, his hands supporting her.

Zadal fisted his cock and prodded her entrance. Gasping, Lindsey slid down slowly. Inch by inch, he parted her depths until she was seated on his hips again.

"Move," Baruk instructed again, rocking her hips the way he wanted.

Lindsey knew this. Knew this all too well and eagerly pushed forward then back, taking Zadal's cock in slow measured strokes. Baruk groaned and pressed his chest to her back. His hands smoothed over her backside as he parted her butt cheeks. Pressure at her rear opening had Lindsey leaning forward. She pressed her face close to Zadal, his lids half closed as he kissed her.

"Let him in, Lindsey."

Wet trickled between her thighs. The tip pierced her hole as Baruk worked his way inside. She knew the moment he was all the way in by the mutual groan they released and the full sensation zinging bursts of pleasure up her spine. Frantic, Lindsey rose up and down on Zadal's shaft. Each stroke sending Baruk in and out at her rear.

It wasn't long before they were moaning and muttering under their breath. Zadal gripped her hair and wrapped the strands about his fingers. Tingles rolled across her scalp and Lindsey's throat locked. Rough and coarse, she reacted to his powerful touch.

"Beautiful. Beautiful and tight." Baruk continued to encourage her to move faster with his hands about her hips.

Her internal muscles clamped down. The dual penetration pinching with bites of pain but her clit swelling with bolts of pleasure.

"I'm going to come," she warned in a breathless gasp.

Zadal yanked her close, breasts smashed against his chest. Strain visible on his face, he thrust up into her harder. "Now. Come now, Lindsey."

Lindsey cried out, her fingers curling into the sheets as she tossed her head. Zadal's hold on her hair meant she felt the tugs on the roots with each twist. Rolling like a storm about to crash through the heavens, she screamed as her climax hit.

Baruk grunted behind her, pounding into her. His breath puffed against her shoulder until he arched up and growled his release.

"Lindsey!" Zadal roared. His seed spurted inside of her as Lindsey collapsed onto his chest.

Heart pounding and sucking air into her lungs, Lindsey said, "You're important, Zadal."

He stiffened beneath her, hands loosening their grip to caress her cheek.

Chapter 7

Zadal didn't knock as he entered Baruk's home office. For once, his spouse partner was alone and his assistant wasn't with him. Baruk glanced up and waved his hand to close his holo-screens. He leaned back in his seat and folded his hands together.

The smug look was enough. Zadal slammed the door behind him. "Your mother contacted me."

Baruk smirked. "Did she?"

Zadal pushed back his anger. "She wanted to thank me for assisting at the mine."

"She's kind that way."

Sofia Laars was indeed kind. Zadal wasn't used to that from a maternal figure. His own mother hadn't wanted him and made sure he knew it every day of his existence.

"You put her up to it," Zadal accused, regaining his annoyance.

Baruk dropped his hands to his lap. "Please tell me what I have put my mother up to?"

Zadal hesitated, doubt causing him to waver. "She has gifted me two companies from the Laars family holdings."

At his announcement, Baruk lost his composure and started to laugh. It wasn't the polite laugh he used at political functions they attended together. It was rich and full. Zadal rolled his eyes and dropped into one of the chairs in front of Baruk's desk.

"What am I to do?" he asked.

Baruk understood Zadal struggled sometimes with his new found wealth. He had plenty on his own but nothing compared to Baruk's family who was one of the richest on Garulax.

"Did you refuse?" Baruk wiped tears from his eyes when he had his mirth under control.

"Of course not! She's also informed me that her next creation will be *the Zadal.*" Baruk's mother was dainty and polite. As a gifted and noted botanist on their world, it would have been an insult to deny her.

"A plant and more businesses. Whatever will you do?"

Zadal should have known he wouldn't get any sympathy. He slouched in the chair, wondering how he could recoup the footing he felt like he'd lost.

The door opened behind him and Zadal knew without turning who was coming in. He turned and watched their wife come in with a baby in each arm. Graeme followed behind with the third. Graeme eyed Lindsey and she nodded toward Zadal. Before he could speak, he had an armful of his precious daughter and the door closed behind Graeme.

Lindsey crossed to the desk but Baruk was already on his feet, hands eager to accept the daughter she gave him. Zadal checked the embroidered C on the tiny top. He held Camille. She punched a tiny fist in the air.

Lindsey marched back toward Zadal, rocking the baby in her arms. "Enough is enough."

He frowned at the severity of her tone. Maybe the babies were tiring her out. "What is wrong?"

"Baruk told me you wanted him to leave you."

The mine. This was about the accident at the mine last week. "Leaving would have been the smart thing to do."

"I would have lost a husband!" her voice got louder, startling Camille.

Zadal shifted her to his shoulder, his palm secure on her back. It had taken him a while to get comfortable handling them but now he did it with ease. "You would have still had Baruk."

She glared. "What about the girls? Don't you care that they wouldn't have had you in their lives?"

Zadal flinched. His family meant *everything* to him. He'd never had one and appreciated them all the more because of that. "Baruk—"

"It's not about Baruk," she cut in. "We are a family. All of us. You're as important as any member."

Zadal swallowed, meeting Baruk's gaze. His spouse partner left him alone to defend himself against Lindsey's ire. Zadal rose. "That's not true."

"I love you." She came closer and leaned into his side, the baby held securely in her arm. "I need you to believe that."

He did. Sometimes. At others, he wondered how he could have been this lucky. He worried she'd regret her choice to have him in her Triad.

"You're not just a spouse partner, Zadal. You're my friend. And you're family."

Zadal's head jerked up at Baruk's words. They'd grown close. They got along. After Lindsey's disappearance, they'd admitted their feelings for her but neither of them had delved into the relationship between them.

"You consider me family?" Zadal asked.

Baruk snorted. "Why else would I carry your heavy ass out of that mine?"

"Baruk!" Lindsey turned her glare on him.

Zadal laughed. He looped his free arm about Lindsey's waist and kissed her long and deep. "Thank you."

For loving him and for a strange Earth woman making him a part of her Triad. Because of Lindsey, he had a family.

Author's Note

Catching up with this trio was fun. I always wanted to know more about Lindsey, Baruk and Zadal. How did they get along after she returned home? In Kyele's Passion, we get a glimpse of her with her husbands and the kids but it was such a teaser and didn't tell me enough about how they'd managed. I've also received email requests about more ménages or more Lindsey. I still say writing ménages are hard. LOL.

Hopefully, this will satisfy some of the curiosity about these three. For Lindsey's full story, it can be found in Lindsey's Rescue.

Want a sneak peak at Bane's book? Turn, swipe and all that good stuff for an exclusive look at the next A World Beyond novel.

Happy Reading,
Michelle H.

Bane's Heart-excerpt

Coming February 2020

Bane listened to the medics, the words they said...and the ones left unspoken. He kept his face blank, not giving away any sign of the growing panic. Week after week, he'd been here. The research center was known for its advanced work on cybernetic enhancements and computronics.

After a mission took a turn sideways, Bane had received necessary cybernetic implants in both of his legs. It was tech deemed outdated and faulty but a desperate resort for him due to the severe nature of his injuries. The team medic, Dr. Maku, had been quite clear when they spoke before Bane's surgery.

"More advanced techniques have been in place but none of them would work with an individual who has sustained your level of nerve impact or in your position."

Cybernetic implants required a chip in his brain and his legs which after therapy and rehab would enable him to control their movement seamlessly. Newer technology required complete replacement of the damaged nerves and had a seventy-eight percent success rate.

Complete replacement would also end his career in the military with the Jutak warriors because those successful patients reported sporadic spasms that had yet to be controlled without extensive medication.

Bane glanced down at his stretched out limbs beneath the pale blue sheet he'd tossed over his lap. This had been his only option and even now it was a failure.

"Do you understand what we have explained, Jutak Hardusho?"

Bane sighed and slumped back against the pillows of the bed he'd already spent more time in then he cared to track. "Yes. I'm fucked."

The head medic, Tao flinched, his smile strained. "That is not how I would say it but there is no medical reason we can find for why your computronics aren't syncing in order for you to walk again."

Turning his head to the side, Bane stared at the wall and ignored the rest of what the three medics added. After a moment of silence they eventually left, closing the door quietly behind them. Bane clenched his fist on his lap, fighting back the need to roar his denial of his circumstances.

It took longer than he wanted to regain control. Taking a deep breath, he grasped the portable comm next to him and contacted a number he'd know in his sleep.

"Hunter's on his way. Estimated arrival three days," Jaron stated without a greeting.

A small smile curled Bane's lips. Forget what medics said. His teammates and friends were the ones Bane counted on. They'd never let him down and they wouldn't now.

About the Author

USA Best Selling Author, Michelle Howard dreamed of writing since reading her first romance novel many years ago but never thought it was possible. Now, she couldn't be happier. She loves paranormal and contemporary romances and is a fan of the classic romances by Judith McNaught, Julie Garwood and a host of others.

I love to hear from fans so please reach out to me. If the mood hits you, leave a review.

Email: michellehowardwrites@gmail.com
Twitter: @mhowardwrites
Instagram: mhowardwrites
Website: www.michellehowardwrites.com
Sign up for my newsletter via my blog

Also by Michelle Howard

A Novel of the Dracol
Rylin's Fire
Relentless Fire
Frost Fire
Secret Fire

Assassins Guild
The Unexpected Bonding Vow
Claiming His Unexpected Baby
His Unexpected Mate

A World Beyond
Torkel's Chosen
Torkels Auserwählte
Arak's Love
Arak's Liebe
Lindsey's Rescue
Kyele's Passion

Rydak's Fall
Jaron's Promise
V'hor's Nestmate
Stolen Moments
Bane's Heart
Nikol's Surrender

Cyborg Redemption
His Cold Kiss
Her Cold Heart

Ghost Unit
Raging Tempest
Craving Love

Le Cœur dans les étoiles
Union à tout prix
Amour à toute épreuve

Liebe in den Sternen
Animalische Begierde
Einzigartige Liebe

Love in the Stars
Mating Urge
Love Like No Other

Magical Lovers
Djinn Lover
Wicked Lover
Wild Lover

The Vassi Contact
As Darkness Spreads
As Dawn Rises

Un roman de L'univers Dracol
La Flamme de Rylin
La Flamme verte
La Flamme de glace

Un Roman di Dracol
il fuoco di Rylin
Fuoco Implacabile
Fuoco di Ghiaccio

Warlord Series
Honor Bound
The Overlord's Heir
A King's Revenge
Rise of the Shadow Warriors
A Warlord's Heart
Unexpected Bride
Unleashing A Warrior

Wired
Wired for Love

Standalone
No Reason To Run
Project Genesis

Watch for more at www.michellehowardwrites.com.